... very ... of all paranoid S...
The E...

'The most clever and riveting vampire novel since *Dracula*'

Dean Koontz

'An inspiration to me'

Stephen King

'A thoughtful, meditative exploration of solitude and despair . . . scary, thrilling, tragic, witty and – ultimately – uplifting'

James Lovegrove

'One of the most important writers of the twentieth century'

Ray Bradbury

'Matheson inspires, it's as simple as that'

Brian Lumley

I Am Legend

RICHARD MATHESON

First published in Great Britain in 1999 by
Millennium
An imprint of Orion Books Ltd

This edition published in Great Britain in 2010 by
Gollancz
An imprint of the Orion Publishing Group
Orion House, 5 Upper St Martin's Lane,
London WC2H 9EA
An Hachette UK company

17 19 20 18 16

A CIP catalogue record for this book
is available from the British Library

ISBN 978 0 575 09416 1

Typeset at The Spartan Press Ltd,
Lymington, Hants

Printed and bound in Great Britain by Clays Ltd, Elcograf S.p.A.

The Orion Publishing Group's policy is to use papers that
are natural, renewable and recyclable products and made
from wood grown in sustainable forests. The logging and
manufacturing processes are expected to conform to the
environmental regulations of the country of origin.

www.orionbooks.co.uk

*To Henry Kuttner with my grateful thanks for
his help and encouragement on this book*

INTRODUCTION

I Am Legend (1954) may be one of the simplest of great SF novels – simplest, at least, in its premise if not the working-out of that premise. The book's central idea is spelt out in the first few pages: Robert Neville, the protagonist, is the only human left alive in a world otherwise inhabited by vampires. The vampires, like those of mythology, are vulnerable to garlic, daylight, and wooden stakes, but not much else. The setting is Los Angeles, beginning in 1976. What's distinctive and unforgettable about the story, though, is the portrait of Neville, the solitary and unwilling hero, fighting his tiny corner with grim determination.

It was Richard Matheson's first novel. He had come to rapid prominence in the SF field in with his early stories (collected in *Born of Man and Woman* (1954)). As with *I Am Legend*, later works like *The Incredible Shrinking Man* (1957) and 'Duel' (1971, also filmed by Steven Spielberg), pit a lonely protagonist against a vast elemental force.

'One man against the world' stories will always tend towards making the protagonist seem a paranoid victim, even when the threat is as objective as the vampires in this book. One of the great successes of *I Am Legend* is that it manages to retain a sense of Robert Neville as a believable person. The little island of humanity he has carved out for himself is meticulously described – the music he listens to, his pleasure in food and drink. Carefully weighted flashbacks give an insight into his life before the vampires came, and a sense that he could be anyone. At the same time, the book makes clear his extra-ordinary drive both to survive and to make sense of his predicament. (In that respect, it's also a cousin of modern zombie films such as *28 Days Later* (2002), whose shambling hordes have the same implacability as Matheson's vampires.) Matheson carefully balances Neville's moments of reflection with jolts of tension and superbly-written action set pieces.

It'd be a fruitless debate to argue whether *I Am Legend* is 'really' horror or science fiction. On the one hand, vampires come from the horror tradition, and some of the set pieces are clearly meant to make the reader terrified as horror stories do. On the other, the book is set over 20 years after its date of publication, and one of the things it does is to try to decouple vampires from the Dracula story and present them in a modern light. The book partakes of both traditions, and plenty of other revisionist vampire stories have done similar things – for instance, Brian Stableford's *The Empire of Fear* (1988), and Dan Simmons's *Carrion Comfort* (1989). But it's worth emphasising how much it makes the vampires subject to the rules of rationality. Neville can deduce things about them, and so help himself. This is a very characteristic move of science fiction: the idea that the universe can be made sense of if studied with sufficient care. (One turning-point of the book is Neville going to the deserted Los Angeles Public Library: from that point on, you feel, the vampire story is going to be explicable in certain ways.)

For much of its length *I Am Legend* focuses, as it has to, on Robert Neville. The story broadens a little in the last third and then, in its final pages, it takes a mythic turn. Having, for almost all the story, been told from the perspective of Neville on his own, there's a sudden reversal of viewpoint. It puts a new light on Neville's burning desire to survive, and the fact that he's killed many of the vampires – some out of self-defence, some not. The solipsism he's lived in for so long is shattered. The ending is probably the inevitable one for a story like this, but it's unforgettably executed. A simple story has become more complex; both Neville and the reader are granted a new perspective; and *I Am Legend* earns its title. The book shuts like a trap: it may be simple, but it's also definitive.

Graham Sleight,
August 2009

PART 1: JANUARY 1976

CHAPTER ONE

On those cloudy days, Robert Neville was never sure when sunset came, and sometimes they were in the streets before he could get back.

If he had been more analytical, he might have calculated the approximate time of their arrival; but he still used the lifetime habit of judging nightfall by the sky, and on cloudy days that method didn't work. That was why he chose to stay near the house on those days.

He walked around the house in the dull gray of afternoon, a cigarette dangling from the corner of his mouth, trailing threadlike smoke over his shoulder. He checked each window to see if any of the boards had been loosened. After violent attacks, the planks were often split or partially pried off, and he had to replace them completely; a job he hated. Today only one plank was loose. Isn't that amazing? he thought.

In the back yard he checked the hothouse and the water tank. Sometimes the structure around the tank might be weakened or its rain catchers bent or broken off. Sometimes they would lob rocks over the high fence around the hothouse, and occasionally they would tear through the overhead net and he'd have to replace panes.

Both the tank and the hothouse were undamaged today.

He went to the house for a hammer and nails. As he pushed open the front door, he looked at the distorted reflection of himself in the cracked mirror he'd fastened to the door a month ago. In a few days, jagged pieces of the silver-backed glass would start to fall off. Let 'em fall, he thought. It was the last damned mirror he'd put there; it wasn't worth it. He'd put garlic there instead. Garlic always worked.

He passed slowly through the dim silence of the living room, turned left into the small hallway, and left again into his bedroom.

Once the room had been warmly decorated, but that was in another time. Now it was a room entirely functional, and since Neville's bed and bureau took up so little space, he had converted one side of the room into a shop.

A long bench covered almost an entire wall, on its hardwood top a heavy band saw, a wood lathe, an emery wheel, and a vise. Above it, on the wall, were haphazard racks of the tools that Robert Neville used.

He took a hammer from the bench and picked out a few nails from one of the disordered bins. Then he went back outside and nailed the plank fast to the shutter. The unused nails he threw into the rubble next door.

For a while he stood on the front lawn looking up and down the silent length of Cimarron Street. He was a tall man, thirty-six, born of English-German stock, his features undistinguished except for the long, determined mouth and the bright blue of his eyes, which moved now over the charred ruins of the houses on each side of his. He'd burned them down to prevent *them* from jumping on his roof from the adjacent ones.

After a few minutes he took a long, slow breath and went back into the house. He tossed the hammer on the living-room couch, then lit another cigarette and had his midmorning drink.

Later he forced himself into the kitchen to grind up the five-day accumulation of garbage in the sink. He knew he should burn up the paper plates and utensils too, and dust the furniture and wash out the sinks and the bathtub and toilet, and change the sheets and pillowcase on his bed; but he didn't feel like it.

For he was a man and he was alone and these things had no importance to him.

It was almost noon. Robert Neville was in his hothouse collecting a basketful of garlic.

In the beginning it had made him sick to smell garlic in such quantity; his stomach had been in a state of constant turmoil. Now the smell was in his house and in his clothes, and sometimes he thought it was even in his flesh. He hardly noticed it at all.

When he had enough bulbs, he went back to the house and dumped them on the drainboard of the sink. As he flicked the wall switch, the light flickered, then flared into normal brilliance. A disgusted hiss passed his clenched teeth. The generator was at it again. He'd have to get out that damned manual again and check the wiring. And, if it were too much trouble to repair, he'd have to install a new generator.

Angrily he jerked a high-legged stool to the sink, got a knife, and sat down with an exhausted grunt.

First he separated the bulbs into the small, sickle-shaped cloves. Then he cut each pink, leathery clove in half, exposing the fleshy center buds. The air thickened with the musky, pungent odor. When it got too oppressive, he snapped on the air-conditioning unit and suction drew away the worst of it.

Now he reached over and took an icepick from its wall rack. He punched holes in each clove half, then strung them all together with wire until he had about twenty-five necklaces.

In the beginning he had hung these necklaces over the windows. But from a distance they'd thrown rocks until he'd been forced to cover the broken panes with plywood scraps. Finally one day he'd torn off the plywood and nailed up even rows of planks instead. It had made the house a gloomy sepulcher, but it was better than having rocks come flying into his rooms in a shower of splintered glass. And, once he had installed the three air-conditioning units, it wasn't too bad. A man could get used to anything if he had to.

When he was finished stringing the garlic cloves, he went

outside and nailed them over the window boarding, taking down the old strings, which had lost most of their potent smell.

He had to go through this process twice a week. Until he found something better, it was his first line of defense.

Defense? he often thought. For what?

All afternoon he made stakes.

He lathed them out of thick doweling, band-sawed into nine-inch lengths. These he held against the whirling emery stone until they were as sharp as daggers.

It was tiresome, monotonous work, and it filled the air with hot-smelling wood dust that settled in his pores and got into his lungs and made him cough.

Yet he never seemed to get ahead. No matter how many stakes he made, they were gone in no time at all. Doweling was getting harder to find, too. Eventually he'd have to lathe down rectangular lengths of wood. Won't *that* be fun? he thought irritably.

It was all very depressing and it made him resolve to find a better method of disposal. But how could he find it when they never gave him a chance to slow down and think?

As he lathed, he listened to records over the loudspeaker he'd set up in the bedroom – Beethoven's Third, Seventh, and Ninth symphonies. He was glad he'd learned early in life, from his mother, to appreciate this kind of music. It helped to fill the terrible void of hours.

From four o'clock on, his gaze kept shifting to the clock on the wall. He worked in silence, lips pressed into a hard line, a cigarette in the corner of his mouth, his eyes staring at the bit as it gnawed away the wood and sent floury dust filtering down to the floor.

Four-fifteen. Four-thirty. It was a quarter to five.

In another hour they'd be at the house again, the filthy bastards. As soon as the light was gone.

He stood before the giant freezer, selecting his supper. His jaded eyes moved over the stacks of meats down to the frozen

4

vegetables, down to the breads and pastries, the fruits and ice cream.

He picked out two lamb chops, string beans, and a small box of orange sherbet. He picked the boxes from the freezer and pushed shut the door with his elbow.

Next he moved over to the uneven stacks of cans piled to the ceiling. He took down a can of tomato juice, then left the room that had once belonged to Kathy and now belonged to his stomach.

He moved slowly across the living room, looking at the mural that covered the back wall. It showed a cliff edge, sheering off to green-blue ocean that surged and broke over black rocks. Far up in the clear blue sky, white sea gulls floated on the wind, and over on the right a gnarled tree hung over the precipice, its dark branches etched against the sky.

Neville walked into the kitchen and dumped the groceries on the table, his eyes moving to the clock. Twenty minutes to six. Soon now.

He poured a little water into a small pan and clanked it down on a stove burner. Next he thawed out the chops and put them under the broiler. By this time the water was boiling and he dropped in the frozen string beans and covered them, thinking that it was probably the electric stove that was milking the generator.

At the table he sliced himself two pieces of bread and poured himself a glass of tomato juice. He sat down and looked at the red second hand as it swept slowly around the clock face. The bastards ought to be here soon.

After he'd finished his tomato juice, he walked to the front door and went out onto the porch. He stepped off onto the lawn and walked down to the sidewalk.

The sky was darkening and it was getting chilly. He looked up and down Cimarron Street, the cool breeze ruffling his blond hair. That's what was wrong with these cloudy days; you never knew when they were coming.

Oh, well, at least they were better than those damned dust

storms. With a shrug, he moved back across the lawn and into the house, locking and bolting the door behind him, sliding the thick bar into place. Then he went back into the kitchen, turned his chops, and switched off the heat under the string beans.

He was putting the food on his plate when he stopped and his eyes moved quickly to the clock. Six-twenty-five today. Ben Cortman was shouting.

'Come out, Neville!'

Robert Neville sat down with a sigh and began to eat.

He sat in the living room, trying to read. He'd made himself a whisky and soda at his small bar and he held the cold glass as he read a physiology text. From the speaker over the hallway door, the music of Schönberg was playing loudly.

Not loudly enough, though. He still heard them outside, their murmuring and their walkings about and their cries, their snarling and fighting among themselves. Once in a while a rock or brick thudded off the house. Sometimes a dog barked.

And they were all there for the same thing.

Robert Neville closed his eyes a moment and held his lips in a tight line. Then he opened his eyes and lit another cigarette, letting the smoke go deep into his lungs.

He wished he'd had time to soundproof the house. It wouldn't be so bad if it weren't that he had to listen to them. Even after five months, it got on his nerves.

He never looked at them any more. In the beginning he'd made a peephole in the front window and watched them. But then the women had seen him and had started striking vile postures in order to entice him out of the house. He didn't want to look at that.

He put down his book and stared bleakly at the rug, hearing *Verklärte Nacht* play over the loud-speaker. He knew he could put plugs in his ears to shut off the sound of them, but that would shut off the music too, and he didn't want to feel that they were forcing him into a shell.

6

He closed his eyes again. It was the women who made it so difficult, he thought, the women posing like lewd puppets in the night on the possibility that he'd see them and decide to come out.

A shudder ran through him. Every night it was the same. He'd be reading and listening to music. Then he'd start to think about soundproofing the house, then he'd think about the women.

Deep in his body, the knotting heat began again, and he pressed his lips together until they were white. He knew the feeling well and it enraged him that he couldn't combat it. It grew and grew until he couldn't sit still any more. Then he'd get up and pace the floor, fists bloodless at his sides. Maybe he'd set up the movie projector or eat something or have too much to drink or turn the music up so loud it hurt his ears. He had to do something when it got really bad.

He felt the muscles of his abdomen closing in like tightening coils. He picked up the book and tried to read, his lips forming each word slowly and painfully.

But in a moment the book was on his lap again. He looked at the bookcase across from him. All the knowledge in those books couldn't put out the fires in him; all the words of centuries couldn't end the wordless, mindless craving of his flesh.

The realization made him sick. It was an insult to a man. All right, it was a natural drive, but there was no outlet for it any more. They'd forced celibacy on him; he'd have to live with it. You have a mind, don't you? he asked himself. Well, *use* it!

He reached over and turned the music still louder, then forced himself to read a whole page without pause. He read about blood cells being forced through membranes, about pale lymph carrying the wastes through tubes blocked by lymph nodes, about lymphocytes and phagocytic cells.

'. . . to empty, in the left shoulder region, near the thorax, into a large vein of the blood circulating system.'

The book shut with a thud.

7

Why didn't they leave him alone? Did they think they could *all* have him? Were they so stupid they thought that? Why did they keep coming every night? After five months, you'd think they'd give up and try elsewhere.

He went over to the bar and made himself another drink. As he turned back to his chair he heard stones rattling down across the roof and landing with thuds in the shrubbery beside the house. Above the noises, he heard Ben Cortman shout as he always shouted.

'Come out, Neville!'

Someday I'll get that bastard, he thought as he took a big swallow of the bitter drink. Someday I'll knock a stake right through his goddamn chest. I'll make one a foot long for him, a special one with ribbons on it, the bastard.

Tomorrow. Tomorrow he'd soundproof the house. His fingers drew into white-knuckled fists. He couldn't stand thinking about those women. If he didn't hear them, maybe he wouldn't think about them. Tomorrow. Tomorrow.

The music ended and he took a stack of records off the turntable and slid them back into their cardboard envelopes. Now he could hear them even more clearly outside. He reached for the first new record he could get and put it on the turntable and twisted the volume up to its highest point.

'The Year of the Plague,' by Roger Leie, filled his ears. Violins scraped and whined, tympani thudded like the beats of a dying heart, flutes played weird, atonal melodies.

With a stiffening of rage, he wrenched up the record and snapped it over his right knee. He'd meant to break it long ago. He walked on rigid legs to the kitchen and flung the pieces into the trash box. Then he stood in the dark kitchen, eyes tightly shut, teeth clenched, hands clamped over his ears. Leave me alone, leave me alone, *leave me alone*!

No use, you couldn't beat them at night. No use trying; it was their special time. He was acting very stupidly, trying to beat them. Should he watch a movie? No, he didn't feel like setting up the projector. He'd go to bed and put the plugs in his ears. It was what he ended up doing every night, anyway.

Quickly, trying not to think at all, he went to the bedroom and undressed. He put on pajama bottoms and went into the bathroom. He never wore pajama tops; it was a habit he'd acquired in Panama during the war.

As he washed, he looked into the mirror at his broad chest, at the dark hair swirling around the nipples and down the center line of his chest. He looked at the ornate cross he'd had tattooed on his chest one night in Panama when he'd been drunk. What a fool I was in those days! he thought. Well, maybe that cross had saved his life.

He brushed his teeth carefully and used dental floss. He tried to take good care of his teeth because he was his own dentist now. Some things could go to pot, but not his health, he thought. Then why don't you stop pouring alcohol into yourself? he thought. Why don't you shut the hell up? he thought.

Now he went through the house, turning out lights. For a few minutes he looked at the mural and tried to believe it was really the ocean. But how could he believe it with all the bumpings and the scrapings, the howlings and snarlings and cries in the night?

He turned off the living-room lamp and went into the bedroom.

He made a sound of disgust when he saw that sawdust covered the bed. He brushed it off with snapping hand strokes, thinking that he'd better build a partition between the shop and the sleeping portion of the room. Better do this and better do that, he thought morosely. There were so many damned things to do, he'd never get to the real problem.

He jammed in his earplugs and a great silence engulfed him. He turned off the light and crawled in between the sheets. He looked at the radium-faced clock and saw that it was only a few minutes past ten. Just as well, he thought. This way I'll get an early start.

He lay there on the bed and took deep breaths of the

darkness, hoping for sleep. But the silence didn't really help. He could still see them out there, the white-faced men prowling around his house, looking ceaselessly for a way to get in at him. Some of them, probably, crouching on their haunches like dogs, eyes glittering at the house, teeth slowly grating together; back and forth, back and forth.

And the women . . .

Did he have to start thinking about *them* again? He tossed over on his stomach with a curse and pressed his face into the hot pillow. He lay there, breathing heavily, body writhing slightly on the sheet. Let the morning come. His mind spoke the words it spoke every night. Dear God, let the morning come.

He dreamed about Virginia and he cried out in his sleep and his fingers gripped the sheets like frenzied talons.

CHAPTER TWO

The alarm went off at five-thirty and Robert Neville reached out a numbed arm in the morning gloom and pushed in the stop.

He reached for his cigarettes and lit one, then sat up. After a few moments he got up and walked into the dark living room and opened the peephole door.

Outside, on the lawn, the dark figures stood like silent soldiers on duty. As he watched, some of them started moving away, and he heard them muttering discontentedly among themselves. Another night was ended.

He went back to the bedroom, switched on the light, and dressed. As he was pulling on his shirt, he heard Ben Cortman cry out, 'Come out, Neville!'

And that was all. After that, they all went away weaker, he knew, than when they had come. Unless they had attacked one of their own. They did that often. There was no union among them. Their need was their only motivation.

After dressing, Neville sat down on his bed with a grunt and penciled his list for the day:

Lathe at Sears
Water
Check generator
Doweling (?)
Usual

Breakfast was hasty: a glass of orange juice, a slice of toast, and two cups of coffee. He finished it quickly, wishing he had the patience to eat slowly.

After breakfast he threw the paper plate and cup into the trash box and brushed his teeth. At least I have one good habit, he consoled himself.

The first thing he did when he went outside was look at the sky. It was clear, virtually cloudless. He could go out today. Good.

As he crossed the porch, his shoe kicked some pieces of the mirror. Well, the damn thing broke just as I thought it would, he thought. He'd clean it up later.

One of the bodies was sprawled on the sidewalk; the other one was half concealed in the shrubbery. They were both women. They were almost always women.

He unlocked the garage door and backed his Willys station wagon into the early-morning crispness. Then he got out and pulled down the back gate. He put on heavy gloves and walked over to the woman on the sidewalk.

There was certainly nothing attractive about them in the daylight, he thought, as he dragged them across the lawn and threw them up on the canvas tarpaulin. There wasn't a drop left in them; both women were the color of fish out of water. He raised the gate and fastened it.

He went around the lawn then, picking up stones and bricks and putting them into a cloth sack. He put the sack in the station wagon and then took off his gloves. He went inside the house, washed his hands, and made lunch: two sandwiches, a few cookies, and a thermos of hot coffee.

When that was done, he went into the bedroom and got his bag of stakes. He slung this across his back and buckled on the holster that held his mallet. Then he went out of the house, locking the front door behind him.

He wouldn't bother searching for Ben Cortman that morning; there were too many other things to do. For a second, he thought about the soundproofing job he'd resolved to do on the house. Well, the hell with it, he thought I'll do it tomorrow or some cloudy day.

He got into the station wagon and checked his list. 'Lathe at Sears'; that was first. After he dumped the bodies, of course.

He started the car and backed quickly into the street and headed for Compton Boulevard. There he turned right and headed east. On both sides of him the houses stood silent, and against the curbs cars were parked, empty and dead.

Robert Neville's eyes shifted down for a moment to the fuel gauge. There was still a half tank, but he might as well stop on Western Avenue and fill it. There was no point in using any of the gasoline stored in the garage until he had to.

He pulled into the silent station and braked. He got a barrel of gasoline and siphoned it into his tank until the pale amber fluid came gushing out of the tank opening and ran down onto the cement.

He checked the oil, water, battery water, and tires. Everything was in good condition. It usually was, because he took special care of the car. If it ever broke down so that he couldn't get back to the house by sunset . . .

Well, there was no point in even worrying about that. If it ever happened, that was the end.

Now he continued up Compton Boulevard past the tall oil derricks, through Compton, through all the silent streets. There was no one to be seen anywhere.

But Robert Neville knew where they were.

The fire was always burning. As the car drew closer, he pulled on his gloves and gas mask and watched through the eyepieces the sooty pall of smoke hovering above the earth. The entire field had been excavated into one gigantic pit; that was in June 1975.

Neville parked the car and jumped out, anxious to get the job over with quickly. Throwing the catch and jerking down the rear gate, he pulled out one of the bodies and dragged it to the edge of the pit. There he stood it on its feet and shoved.

The body bumped and rolled down the steep incline until it settled on the great pile of smoldering ashes at the bottom.

Robert Neville drew in harsh breaths as he hurried back to the station wagon. He always felt as though he were strangling when he was here, even though he had the gas mask on.

Now he dragged the second body to the brink of the pit and pushed it over. Then, after tossing the sack of rocks down, he hurried back to the car and sped away.

After he'd driven a half mile, he skinned off the mask and gloves and tossed them into the back. His mouth opened and he drew in deep lungfuls of the fresh air. He took the flask from the glove compartment and took a long drink of burning whisky. Then he lit a cigarette and inhaled deeply. Sometimes he had to go to the burning pit every day for weeks at a time, and it always made him sick.

Somewhere down there was Kathy.

On the way to Inglewood he stopped at a market to get some bottled water.

As he entered the silent store, the smell of rotted food filled his nostrils. Quickly he pushed a metal wagon up and down the silent, dust-thick aisles, the heavy smell of decay setting his teeth on edge, making him breathe through his mouth.

He found the water bottles in back, and also found a door opening on a flight of stairs. After putting all the bottles into the wagon, he went up the stairs. The owner of the market might be up there; he might as well get started.

There were two of them. In the living room, lying on a couch, was a woman about thirty years old, wearing a red housecoat. Her chest rose and fell slowly as she lay there, eyes closed, her hands clasped over her stomach.

Robert Neville's hands fumbled on the stake and mallet. It was always hard when they were alive; especially with women. He could feel that senseless demand returning again, tightening his muscles. He forced it down. It was insane, there was no rational argument for it.

She made no sound except for a sudden, hoarse intake of

breath. As he walked into the bedroom, he could hear a sound like the sound of water running. Well, what *else* can I do? he asked himself, for he still had to convince himself he was doing the right thing.

He stood in the bedroom doorway, staring at the small bed by the window, his throat moving, breath shuddering in his chest. Then, driven on, he walked to the side of the bed and looked down at her.

Why do they all look like Kathy to me? he thought, drawing out the second stake with shaking hands.

Driving slowly to Sears, he tried to forget by wondering why it was that only wooden stakes should work.

He frowned as he drove along the empty boulevard, the only sound the muted growling of the motor in his car. It seemed fantastic that it had taken him five months to start wondering about it.

Which brought another question to mind. How was it that he always managed to hit the heart? It had to be the heart; Dr Busch had said so. Yet he, Neville, had no anatomical knowledge.

His brow furrowed. It irritated him that he should have gone through this hideous process so long without stopping once to question it.

He shook his head. No, I should think it over carefully, he thought, I should collect all the questions before I try to answer them. Things should be done the right way, the scientific way.

Yeah, yeah, yeah, he thought, shades of old Fritz. That had been his father's name. Neville had loathed his father and fought the acquisition of his father's logic and mechanical facility every inch of the way. His father had died denying the vampire violently to the last.

At Sears he got the lathe, loaded it into the station wagon, then searched the store.

There were five of them in the basement, hiding in various shadowed places. One of them Neville found inside a display freezer. When he saw the man lying there in this enamel coffin, he had to laugh; it seemed such a funny place to hide.

Later, he thought of what a humorless world it was when he could find amusement in such a thing.

About two o'clock he parked and ate his lunch. Everything seemed to taste of garlic.

And that set him wondering about the effect garlic had on them. It must have been the smell that chased them off, but why?

They were strange, the facts about them: their staying inside by day, their avoidance of garlic, their death by stake, their reputed fear of crosses, their supposed dread of mirrors.

Take that last, now. According to legend, they were invisible in mirrors, but he knew that was untrue. As untrue as the belief that they transformed themselves into bats. That was a superstition that logic plus observation had easily disposed of. It was equally foolish to believe that they could transform themselves into wolves. Without a doubt there were vampire dogs; he had seen and heard them outside his house at night. But they were only dogs.

Robert Neville compressed his lips suddenly. Forget it, he told himself; you're not ready yet. The time would come when he'd take a crack at it, detail for detail, but the time wasn't now. There were enough things to worry about now.

After lunch, he went from house to house and used up all his stakes. He had forty-seven stakes.

CHAPTER THREE

'The strength of the vampire is that no one will believe in him.'

Thank *you*. Dr Van Helsing, he thought, putting down his copy of 'Dracula.' He sat staring moodily at the bookcase, listening to Brahms' second piano concerto, a whisky sour in his right hand, a cigarette between his lips.

It was true. The book was a hodgepodge of superstitions and soap-opera clichés, but that line was true; no one had believed in them, and how could they fight something they didn't even believe in?

That was what the situation had been. Something black and of the night had come crawling out of the Middle Ages. Something with no framework or credulity, something that had been consigned, fact and figure, to the pages of imaginative literature. Vampires were passé, Summers' idylls or Stoker's melodramatics or a brief inclusion in the Britannica or grist for the pulp writer's mill or raw material for the B-film factories. A tenuous legend passed from century to century.

Well, it was true.

He took a sip from his drink and closed his eyes as the cold liquid trickled down his throat and warmed his stomach. True, he thought, but no one ever got the chance to know it. Oh, they knew it was something, but it couldn't be that – not *that*. *That* was imagination, *that* was superstition, there was no such thing as *that*.

And, before science had caught up with the legend, the legend had swallowed science and everything.

He hadn't found any doweling that day. He hadn't checked the generator. He hadn't cleaned up the pieces of mirror. He hadn't eaten supper; he'd lost his appetite. That wasn't hard. He lost it most of the time. He couldn't do the things he'd done all afternoon and then come home to a hearty meal. Not even after five months.

He thought of the eleven – no, the twelve children that afternoon, and he finished his drink in two swallows.

He blinked and the room wavered a little before him. You're getting blotto, Father, he told himself. So what? he returned. Has anyone more right?

He tossed the book across the room. Begone, Van Helsing and Mina and Jonathan and blood-eyed Count and all! All figments, all driveling extrapolations on a somber theme.

A coughing chuckle emptied itself from his throat. Outside, Ben Cortman called for him to come out. Be right out, Benny, he thought. Soon as I get my tuxedo on.

He shuddered and gritted his teeth edges together. Be right out. Well, why not? Why *not* go out? It was a sure way to be free of them.

Be one of them.

He chuckled at the simplicity of it, then shoved himself up and walked crookedly to the bar. Why not? His mind plodded on. Why go through all this complexity when a flung-open door and a few steps would end it all?

For the life of him, he didn't know. There was, of course, the faint possibility that others like him existed somewhere, trying to go on, hoping that someday they would be among their own kind again. But how could he ever find them if they weren't within a day's drive of his house?

He shrugged and poured more whisky in the glass; he'd given up the use of jiggers months ago. Garlic on the windows and nets over the hothouse and burn the bodies and cart the rocks away and, fraction of an inch by fraction of an inch, reduce their unholy numbers. Why kid himself? He'd never find anyone else.

His body dropped down heavily on the chair. Here we are, kiddies, sitting like a bug in a rug, snugly, surrounded by a battalion of blood-suckers who wish no more than to sip freely of my bonded, 100-proof hemoglobin. Have a drink, men, this one's really on me.

His face twisted into an expression of raw, unqualified hatred. *Bastards!* I'll kill every mother's son of you before I'll give in! His right hand closed like a clamp and the glass shattered in his grip.

He looked down, dull-eyed, at the fragments on the floor, at the jagged piece of glass still in his hand, at the whisky-diluted blood dripping off his palm.

Wouldn't they like to get some of it, though? he thought. He started up with a furious lurch and almost opened the door so he could wave the hand in their faces and hear them howl.

Then he closed his eyes and a shudder ran through his body. Wise up, buddy, he thought. Go bandage your goddamn hand.

He stumbled into the bathroom and washed his hand carefully, gasping as he daubed iodine into the sliced-open flesh. Then he bandaged it clumsily, his broad chest rising and falling with jerky movements, sweat dripping from his forehead. I need a cigarette, he thought.

In the living room again, he changed Brahms for Bernstein and lit a cigarette. What will I do if I ever run out of coffin nails? he wondered, looking at the cigarette's blue trailing smoke. Well, there wasn't much chance of that. He had about a thousand cartons in the closet of Kathy's—

He clenched his teeth together. In the closet of the *larder*, the *larder*, the *larder*.

Kathy's room.

He sat staring with dead eyes at the mural while 'The Age of Anxiety' pulsed in his ears. Age of anxiety, he mused. You thought you had anxiety, Lenny boy. Lenny and Benny; you two should meet. Composer, meet corpse. Mamma, when I grow up I wanna be a wampir like Dada. Why, bless you, hon, of course you shall.

The whisky gurgled into the glass. He grimaced a little at the pain in his hand and shifted the bottle to his left hand.

He sat down and sipped. Let the jagged edge of sobriety be now dulled, he thought. Let the crumby balance of clear vision be expunged, but post haste. I hate 'em.

Gradually the room shifted on its gyroscopic center and wove and undulated about his chair. A pleasant haze, fuzzy at the edges, took over sight. He looked at the glass, at the record player. He let his head flop from side to side. Outside, they prowled and muttered and waited.

Pore vampires, he thought, pore little cusses, pussy-footin' round my house, so thirsty, so all forlorn.

A thought. He raised a forefinger that wavered before his eyes.

Friends, I come before you to discuss the vampire; a minority element if there ever was one, and there was one.

But to concision: I will sketch out the basis for my thesis, which thesis is this: Vampires are prejudiced against.

The keynote of minority prejudice is this: They are loathed because they are feared. Thus . . .

He made himself a drink. A long one.

At one time, the Dark and Middle Ages, to be succinct, the vampire's power was great, the fear of him tremendous. He was anathema and still remains anathema. Society hates him without ration.

But are his needs any more shocking than the needs of other animals and men? Are his deeds more outrageous than the deeds of the parent who drained the spirit from his child? The vampire may foster quickened heartbeats and levitated hair. But is he worse than the parent who gave to society a neurotic child who became a politician? Is he worse than the manufacturer who set up belated foundations with the money he made by handing bombs and guns to suicidal nationalists? Is he worse than the distiller who gave bastardized grain juice to stultify further the brains of those who, sober, were incapable of a progressive thought? (Nay, I apologize for this calumny; I nip the brew that feeds me.) Is he worse, then, than the publisher who filled ubiquitous racks with lust and death wishes? Really, now, search your soul, lovie – is the vampire so bad?

All he does is drink blood.

Why, then, this unkind prejudice, this thoughtless bias? Why cannot the vampire live where he chooses? Why must he seek out hiding places where none can find him out? Why do you wish him destroyed? Ah, see, you have turned the poor guile-less innocent into a haunted animal. He has no means of support, no measures for proper education, he has not the voting franchise. No wonder he is compelled to seek out a predatory nocturnal existence.

Robert Neville grunted a surly grunt. Sure, sure, he thought, but would you let your sister marry one?

He shrugged. You got me there, buddy, you got me there.

The music ended. The needle scratched back and forth in the black grooves. He sat there, feeling a chill creeping up his legs. That's what was wrong with drinking too much. You became immune to drunken delights. There was no solace in liquor. Before you got happy, you collapsed. Already the room was straightening out, the sounds outside were starting to nibble at his eardrums.

'Come out, Neville!'

His throat moved and a shaking breath passed his lips. Come out. The women were out there, their dresses open or taken off, their flesh waiting for his touch, their lips waiting for—

My blood, my *blood*!

As if it were someone else's hand, he watched his whitened fist rise up slowly, shuddering, to drive down on his leg. The pain made him suck in a breath of the house's stale air. Garlic. Everywhere the smell of garlic. In his clothes and in the furniture and in his food and even in his drink. Have a garlic and soda; his mind rattled out the attempted joke.

He lurched up and started pacing. What am I going to do

now? Go through the routine again? I'll save you the trouble. Reading-drinking-soundproof-the-house – the women. The women, the lustful, bloodthirsty, naked women flaunting their hot bodies at him. No, not hot.

A shuddering whine wrenched up through his chest and throat. Goddamn them, what were they waiting for? Did they think he was going to come out and hand himself over?

Maybe I am, maybe I am. He actually found himself jerking off the crossbar from the door. Coming, girls, I'm coming. Wet your lips, now.

Outside, they heard the bar being lifted, and a howl of anticipation sounded in the night.

Spinning, he drove his fists one after the other into the wall until he'd cracked the plaster and broken his skin. Then he stood there trembling helplessly, his teeth chattering.

After a while it passed. He put the bar back across the door and went into the bedroom. He sank down on the bed and fell back on the pillow with a groan. His left hand beat once, feebly, on the bedspread.

Oh, *God*, he thought, how long, how long?

CHAPTER FOUR

The alarm never went off because he'd forgotten to set it. He slept soundly and motionlessly, his body like cast iron. When he finally opened his eyes, it was ten o'clock.

With a disgusted muttering, he struggled up and dropped his legs over the side of the bed. Instantly his head began throbbing as if his brains were trying to force their way through his skull. Fine, he thought, a hangover. That's all I need.

He pushed himself up with a groan and stumbled into the bathroom, threw water in his face and splashed some over his head. No good, his mind complained, no good. I still feel like hell. In the mirror his face was gaunt, bearded, and very much like the face of a man in his forties. Love, your magic spell is everywhere; inanely, the words flapped across his brain like wet sheets in a wind.

He walked slowly into the living room and opened the front door. A curse fell thickly from his lips at the sight of the woman crumpled across the sidewalk. He started to tighten angrily, but it made his head throb too much and he had to let it go. I'm sick, he thought.

The sky was gray and dead. Great! he thought. Another day stuck in this boarded-up rat hole! He slammed the door viciously, then winced, groaning, at the brain-stabbing noise. Outside, he heard the rest of the mirror fall out and shatter on the porch cement. Oh, *great*! His lips contorted back into a white twist of flesh.

Two cups of burning black coffee only made his stomach

feel worse. He put down the cup and went into the living room. To hell with it, he thought, I'll get drunk again.

But the liquor tasted like turpentine, and with a rasping snarl he flung the glass against the wall and stood watching the liquor run down onto the rug. Hell, I'm runnin' out of glasses. The thought irritated him while breath struggled in through his nostrils and out again in faltering bursts.

He sank down on the couch and sat there, shaking his head slowly. It was no use; they'd beaten him, the black bastards had beaten him.

That restless feeling again; the feeling as if he were expanding and the house were contracting and any second now he'd go bursting through its frame in an explosion of wood, plaster, and brick. He got up and moved quickly to the door, his hands shaking.

On the lawn, he stood sucking in great lungfuls of the wet morning air, his face turned away from the house he hated. But he hated the other houses around there too, and he hated the pavement and the sidewalks and the lawns and everything that was on Cimarron Street.

It kept building up. And suddenly he knew he had to get out of there. Cloudy day or not, he had to get out of there.

He locked the front door, unlocked the garage, and dragged up the thick door on its overhead hinges. He didn't bother putting down the door. I'll be back soon, he thought. I'll just go away for a while.

He backed the station wagon quickly down the driveway, jerked it around, and pressed down hard on the accelerator, heading for Compton Boulevard. He didn't know where he was going.

He went around the corner doing forty and jumped that to sixty-five before he'd gone another block. The car leaped forward under his foot and he kept the accelerator on the floor, forced down by a rigid leg. His hands were like carved ice on the wheel and his face was the face of a statue. At eighty-nine miles an hour, he shot down the lifeless, empty boulevard, one roaring sound in the great stillness.

Things rank and gross in nature possess it merely, he thought as he walked slowly across the cemetery lawn.

The grass was so high that the weight of it had bent it over and it crunched under his heavy shoes as he walked. There was no sound but that of his shoes and the now senseless singing of birds. Once I thought they sang because everything was right with the world, Robert Neville thought. I know now I was wrong. They sing because they're feeble-minded.

He had raced six miles, the gas pedal pressed to the floor, before he'd realized where he was going. It was strange the way his mind and body had kept it secret from his consciousness. Consciously, he'd known only that he was sick and depressed and had to get away from the house. He didn't know he was going to visit Virginia.

But he'd driven there directly and as fast as he could. He'd parked at the curb and entered through the rusted gate, and now his shoes were pressing and crackling through the thick grass.

How long had it been since he'd come here? It must have been at least a month. He wished he'd brought flowers, but then, he hadn't realized he was coming here until he was almost at the gate.

His lips pressed together as an old sorrow held him again. Why couldn't he have Kathy there too? Why had he followed so blindly, listening to those fools who set up their stupid regulations during the plague? If only she could be there, lying across from her mother.

Don't start that again, he ordered himself.

Drawing closer to the crypt, he stiffened as he noticed that the iron door was slightly ajar. Oh, *no*, he thought. He broke into a run across the wet grass. If they've been at her, I'll burn down the city, he vowed. I swear to God, I'll burn it to the ground if they've touched her.

He flung open the door and it clanged against the marble

wall with a hollow, echoing sound. His eyes moved quickly to the marble base on which the sealed casket rested.

The tension sank; he drew in breath again. It was still there, untouched.

Then, as he started in, he saw the man lying in one corner of the crypt, body curled up on the cold floor.

With a grunt of rage, Robert Neville rushed at the body, and, grabbing the man's coat in taut fingers, he dragged him across the floor and flung him violently out onto the grass. The body rolled onto its back, the white face pointing at the sky.

Robert Neville went back into the crypt, chest rising and falling with harsh movements. Then he closed his eyes and stood with his palms resting on the cover of the casket.

I'm here, he thought. I'm back. Remember me.

He threw out the flowers he'd brought the time before and cleared away the few leaves that had blown in because the door had been opened.

Then he sat down beside the casket and rested his forehead against its cold metal side.

Silence held him in its cold and gentle hands.

If I could die now, he thought; peacefully, gently, without a tremor or a crying out. If I could be with her. If I could believe I would be with her.

His fingers tightened slowly and his head sank forward on his chest.

Virginia. Take me where you are.

A tear, crystal, fell across his motionless hand . . .

He had no idea how long he'd been there. After a while, though, even the deepest sorrow faltered, even the most penetrating despair lost its scalpel edge. The flagellant's curse, he thought, to grow inured even to the whip.

He straightened up and stood. Still alive, he thought, heart beating senselessly, veins running without point, bones and muscles and tissue all alive and functioning with no purpose at all.

A moment longer he stood looking down at the casket, then he turned away with a sigh and left, closing the door behind him quietly so as not to disturb her sleep.

He'd forgotten about the man. He almost tripped over him now, stepping aside with a muttered curse and starting past the body.

Then, abruptly, he turned back.

What's this? He looked down incredulously at the man. The man was dead; really dead. But how could that be? The change had occurred so quickly, yet already the man looked and smelled as though he'd been dead for days.

His mind began churning with a sudden excitement. Something had killed the vampire; something brutally effective. The heart had not been touched, no garlic had been present, and yet . . .

It came, seemingly, without effort. Of course – the daylight!

A bolt of self-accusation struck him. To know for five months that they remained indoors by day and never *once* to make the connection! He closed his eyes, appalled by his own stupidity.

The rays of the sun; the infrared and ultraviolet. It had to be them. But why? Damn it, why didn't he know anything about the effects of sunlight on the human system?

Another thought: That man had been one of the true vampires; the living dead. Would sunlight have the same effect on those who were still alive?

The first excitement he'd felt in months made him break into a run for the station wagon.

As the door slammed shut beside him, he wondered if he should have taken away the dead man. Would the body attract others, would they invade the crypt? No, they wouldn't go near the casket, anyway; it was sealed with garlic. Besides, the man's blood was dead now, it—

Again his thoughts broke off as he leaped to another conclusion. The sun's rays must have done something to their blood!

Was it possible, then, that all things bore relation to the blood? The garlic, the cross, the mirror, the stake, daylight, the earth some of them slept in? He didn't see how, and yet . . .

He had to do a lot of reading, a lot of research. It might be just the thing he needed. He'd been planning for a long time to do it, but lately it seemed as if he'd forgotten it altogether. Now this new idea started the desire again.

He started the car and raced up the street, turning off into a residential section and pulling up before the first house he came to.

He ran up the pathway to the front door, but it was locked and he couldn't force it in. With an impatient growl, he ran to the next house. The door was open and he ran to the stairs through the darkened living room and jumped up the carpeted steps two at a time.

He found the woman in the bedroom. Without hesitation, he jerked back the covers and grabbed her by the wrists. She grunted as her body hit the floor, and he heard her making tiny sounds in her throat as he dragged her into the hall and started down the stairs.

As he pulled her across the living room, she started to move.

Her hands closed over his wrists and her body began to twist and flop on the rug. Her eyes were still closed, but she gasped and muttered and her body kept trying to writhe out of his grip. Her dark nails dug into his flesh. He tore out of her grasp with a snarl and dragged her the rest of the way by her hair. Usually he felt a twinge when he realized that, but for some affliction he didn't understand, these people were the same as he. But now an experimental fervor had seized him and he could think of nothing else.

Even so, he shuddered at the strangled sound of horror she made when he threw her on the sidewalk outside.

She lay twisting helplessly on the sidewalk, hands opening and closing, lips drawn back from red-spotted lips. Robert Neville watched her tensely.

His throat moved. It wouldn't last, the feeling of callous brutality. He bit his lips as he watched her. All right, she's suffering, he argued with himself, but she's one of them and she'd kill me gladly if she got the chance. You've got to look at it that way, it's the only way. Teeth clenched, he stood there and watched her die.

In a few minutes she stopped moving, stopped muttering, and her hands uncurled slowly like white blossoms on the cement. Robert Neville crouched down and felt for her heartbeat. There was none. Already her flesh was growing cold.

He straightened up with a thin smile. It was true, then. He didn't need the stakes. After all this time, he'd finally found a better method.

Then his breath caught. But how did he know the woman was really dead? How could he know until sunset?

The thought filled him with a new, more restless anger. Why did each question blight the answers before it?

He thought about it as he sat drinking a can of tomato juice taken from the supermarket behind which he was parked.

How was he going to know? He couldn't very well stay with the woman until sunset came.

Take her home with you, fool.

Again his eyes closed and he felt a shudder of irritation go through him. He was missing all the obvious answers today. Now he'd have to go all the way back and find her, and he wasn't even sure where the house was.

He started the motor and pulled away from the parking lot, glancing down at his watch. Three o'clock. Plenty of time to get back before they came. He eased the gas pedal down and the station wagon pulled ahead faster.

It took him about a half hour to relocate the house. The woman was still in the same position on the sidewalk. Putting on his gloves, Neville lowered the back gate of the station wagon and walked over to the woman. As he walked, he noticed her figure. No, don't start that again, for God's sake.

He dragged the woman back to the station wagon and tossed her in. Then he closed the gate and took off his gloves. He held up the watch and looked at it. Three o'clock. Plenty of time to—

He jerked up the watch and held it against his ear, his heart suddenly jumping.

The watch had stopped.

CHAPTER FIVE

His fingers shook as he turned the ignition key. His hands gripped the wheel rigidly as he made a tight U turn and started back toward Gardena.

What a fool he'd been! It must have taken at least an hour to reach the cemetery. He must have been in the crypt for hours. Then going to get that woman. Going to the market, drinking the tomato juice, going back to get the woman again.

What time *was* it?

Fool! Cold fear poured through his veins at the thought of them all waiting for him at his house. Oh, my God, and he'd left the garage door open! The gasoline, the equipment – *the generator*!

A groan cut itself off in his throat as he jammed the gas pedal to the floor and the small station wagon leaped ahead, the speedometer needle fluttering, then moving steadily past the sixty-five mark, the seventy, the seventy-five. What if they were already waiting for him? How could he possibly get in the house?

He forced himself to be calm. He musn't go to pieces now; he had to keep himself in check. He'd get in. Don't worry, you'll get inside, he told himself. But he didn't see how.

One hand ran nervously through his hair. This is fine, fine, commented his mind. You go to all that trouble to preserve your existence, and then one day you just don't come back in time. Shut up! his mind snapped back at itself. But he could have killed himself for forgetting to wind his watch the night before.

Don't bother killing yourself, his mind reflected, they'll be glad to do it for you. Suddenly he realized he was almost weak from hunger. The small amount of canned meat he'd eaten with the tomato juice had done nothing to alleviate hunger.

The silent streets flew past and he kept looking from side to side to see if any of them were appearing in the doorways. It seemed as if it were already getting dark, but that could have been imagination. It couldn't be that late, it couldn't be.

He'd just gone hurtling past the corner of Western and Compton when he saw the man come running out of a building and shout at him. His heart was contracted in an icy hand as the man's cry fluttered in the air behind the car.

He couldn't get any more speed out of the station wagon. And now his mind began torturing him with visions of one of the tires going, the station wagon veering, leaping the curb and crashing into a house. His lips started to shake and he jammed them together to stop them. His hands on the wheel felt numb.

He had to slow down at the corner of Cimarron. Out of the corner of an eye he saw a man come rushing out of a house and start chasing the car.

Then, as he turned the corner with a screech of clinging tires, he couldn't hold back the gasp.

They were all in front of his house, waiting.

A sound of helpless terror filled his throat. He didn't want to die. He might have thought about it, even contemplated it. But he didn't want to die. Not like *this*.

Now he saw them all turn their white faces at the sound of the motor. Some more of them came running out of the open garage and his teeth ground together in impotent fury. What a stupid, brainless way to die!

Now he saw them start running straight toward the station wagon, a line of them across the street. And, suddenly, he knew he couldn't stop. He pressed down on the accelerator, and in a moment the car went plowing through them, knocking three of them aside like tenpins. He felt the car frame jolt as it struck the bodies. Their screaming white faces went flashing by his window, their cries chilling his blood.

Now they were behind and he saw in the rear-view mirror that they were all pursuing him. A sudden plan caught hold in his mind, and impulsively he slowed down, even braking, until the speed of the car fell to thirty, then twenty miles an hour.

He looked back and saw them gaining, saw their grayish-white faces approaching, their dark eyes fastened to his car, to *him*.

Suddenly he twitched with shock as a snarl sounded nearby and, jerking his head around, he saw the crazed face of Ben Cortman beside the car.

Instinctively his foot jammed down on the gas pedal, but his other foot slipped off the clutch, and with a neck-snapping jolt the station wagon jumped forward and stalled.

Sweat broke out on his forehead as he lunged forward feverishly to press the button. Ben Cortman clawed in at him.

With a snarl he shoved the cold white hand aside.

'Neville, Neville!'

Ben Cortman reached in again, his hands like claws cut from ice. Again Neville pushed aside the hand and jabbed at the starter button, his body shaking helplessly. Behind, he could hear them all screaming excitedly as they came closer to the car.

The motor coughed into life again as he felt Ben Cortman's long nails rake across his cheek.

'Neville!'

The pain made his hand jerk into a rigid fist, which he drove into Cortman's face. Cortman went flailing back onto the pavement as the gears caught and the station wagon jolted forward, picking up speed. One of the others caught up and leaped at the rear of the car. For a minute he held on, and Robert Neville could see his ashen face glaring insanely through the back window. Then he jerked the car over toward the curb, swerved sharply, and shook the man off. The man went running across a lawn, arms ahead of him, and smashed violently into the side of a house.

Robert Neville's heart was pounding so heavily now it seemed as if it would drive through his chest walls. Breath shuddered in him and his flesh felt numb and cold. He could feel the trickle of blood on his cheek, but no pain. Hastily he wiped it off with one shaking hand.

Now he spun the station wagon around the corner, turning right He kept looking at the rear-view mirror, then looking ahead. He went the short block to Haas Street and turned right again. What if they cut through the yards and blocked his way?

He slowed down a little until they came swarming around the corner like a pack of wolves. Then he pressed down on the accelerator. He'd have to take the chance that they were all following him. Would some of them guess what he was trying?

He shoved down the gas pedal all the way and the station wagon jumped forward, racing up the block. He wheeled it around the corner at fifty miles an hour, gunned up the short block to Cimarron, and turned right again.

His breath caught. There was no one in sight on his lawn. There was still a chance, then. He'd have to let the station wagon go, though; there was no time to put it in the garage.

He jerked the car to the curb and shoved the door open. As he raced around the edge of the car he heard the billowing cry of their approach around the corner.

He'd have to take a chance on locking the garage. If he didn't, they might destroy the generator; they couldn't have had time to do it already. His footsteps pounded up the driveway to the garage.

'Neville!'

His body jerked back as Cortman came lunging out of the dark shadows of the garage.

Cortman's body drove into his and almost knocked him down. He felt the cold, powerful hands clamp on his throat and smelled the fetid breath clouding over his face. The two of them went reeling back toward the sidewalk and the white-fanged mouth went darting down at Robert Neville's throat.

Abruptly he jerked up his right fist and felt it drive into Cortman's throat. He heard the choking sound in Cortman's throat. Up the block the first of them came rushing and screaming around the corner.

With a violent movement, Robert Neville grabbed Cortman by his long, greasy hair and sent him hurtling down the driveway until he rammed head on into the side of the station wagon.

Robert Neville's eyes flashed up the street. No time for the garage! He dashed around the corner of the house and up to the porch.

He skidded to a halt. Oh, God, the keys!

With a terrified intake of breath he spun and rushed back toward the car. Cortman started up with a throaty snarl and he drove his knee into the white face and knocked Cortman back on the sidewalk. Then he lunged into the car and jerked the key chain away from the ignition slot.

As he scuttled back out of the car the first one of them came leaping at him.

He shrank back onto the car seat and the man tripped over his legs and went sprawling heavily onto the sidewalk. Robert Neville pushed himself out, dashed across the lawn, and leaped onto the porch.

He had to stop to find the right key and another man came leaping up the porch steps. Neville was slammed against the house by the impact of his body. The hot blood-thick breath was on him again, the bared mouth lunging at his throat. He drove his knee into the man's groin and then, leaning his weight against the house, he raised his foot high and shoved the doubled-over man into the other one who was rushing across the lawn.

Neville dived for the door and unlocked it. He pushed it open, slipped inside, and turned. As he slammed it shut an arm shot through the opening. He forced the door against it with all his strength until he heard bones snap, then he opened the door a little, shoved the broken arm out, and slammed the door. With trembling hands he dropped the bar into place.

Slowly he sank down onto the floor and fell on his back. He lay there in the darkness, his chest rising and falling, his legs and arms like dead limbs on the floor. Outside they howled and pummeled the door, shouting his name in a paroxysm of demented fury. They grabbed up bricks and rocks and hurled them against the house and they screamed and cursed at him. He lay there listening to the thud of the rocks and bricks against the house, listening to their howling.

After a while he struggled up to the bar. Half the whisky he poured splashed onto the rug. He threw down the contents of the glass and stood there shivering, holding onto the bar to support his wobbling legs, his throat tight and convulsed, his lips shaking without control.

Slowly the heat of the liquor expanded in his stomach and reached his body. His breath slowed down, his chest stopped shuddering.

He started as he heard the great crash outside.

He ran to the peephole and looked out. His teeth grated together and a burst of rage filled him as he saw the station wagon lying on its side and saw them smashing in the windshield with bricks and stones, tearing open the hood and smashing at the engine with insane club strokes, denting the frame with their frenzied blows. As he watched, fury poured through him like a current of hot acid and half-formed curses sounded in his throat while his hands clamped into great white fists at his sides.

Turning suddenly, he moved to the lamp and tried to light it. It didn't work. With a snarl he turned and ran into the kitchen. The refrigerator was out. He ran from one dark room to another. The freezer was off; all the food would spoil. His house was a dead house.

Fury exploded in him. Enough!

His rage-palsied hands ripped out the clothes from the bureau drawer until they closed on the loaded pistols.

Racing through the dark living room, he knocked up the bar across the door and sent it clattering to the floor. Outside, they howled as they heard him opening the door. I'm coming out, you bastards! his mind screamed out.

He jerked open the door and shot the first one in the face. The man went spinning back off the porch and two women came at him in muddy, torn dresses, their white arms spread to enfold him. He watched their bodies jerk as the bullets struck them, then he shoved them both aside and began firing his guns into their midst, a wild yell ripping back his bloodless lips.

He kept firing the pistols until they were both empty. Then he stood on the porch clubbing them with insane blows, losing his mind almost completely when the same ones he'd shot came rushing at him again. And when they tore the guns out of his hands he used his fists and elbows and he butted with his head and kicked them with his big shoes.

It wasn't until the flaring pain of having his shoulder slashed open struck him that he realized what he was doing and how hopeless his attempt was. Knocking aside two women, he backed toward the door. A man's arm locked around his neck. He lurched forward, bending at the waist, and toppled the man over his head into the others. He jumped back into the doorway, gripped both sides of the frame, and kicked out his legs like pistons, sending the men crashing back into the shrubbery.

Then, before they could get at him again, he slammed the door in their faces, locked it, bolted it, and dropped the heavy bar into its slots.

Robert Neville stood in the cold blackness of his house, listening to the vampires scream.

He stood against the wall clubbing slowly and weakly at the plaster, tears streaming down his bearded cheeks, his bleeding hand pulsing with pain. Everything was gone, everything.

'Virginia,' he sobbed like a lost, frightened child. 'Virginia. *Virginia.*'

PART 2: MARCH 1976

CHAPTER SIX

The house, at last, was livable again.

Even more so than before, in fact, for he had finally taken three days and soundproofed the walls. Now they could scream and howl all they wanted and he didn't have to listen to them. He especially liked not having to listen to Ben Cortman any more.

It had all taken time and work. First of all was the matter of a new car to replace the one they'd destroyed. This had been more difficult than he'd imagined.

He had to get over to Santa Monica to the only Willys store he knew about. The Willys station wagons were the only ones he had had any experience with, and this didn't seem quite the time to start experimenting. He couldn't walk to Santa Monica, so he had to try using one of the many cars parked around the neighborhood. But most of them were inoperative for one reason or another: a dead battery, a clogged fuel pump, no gasoline, flat tires.

Finally, in a garage about a mile from the house, he found a car he could get started, and he drove quickly to Santa Monica to pick up another station wagon. He put a new battery in it, filled its tank with gasoline, put gasoline drums in the back, and drove home. He got back to the house about an hour before sunset.

He made sure of that.

Luckily the generator had not been ruined. The vampires apparently had no idea of its importance to him, for, except for a torn wire and a few cudgel blows, they had left it alone. He'd managed to fix it quickly the morning after the attack and keep his frozen foods from spoiling. He was grateful for that, because he was sure there were no places left where he could get more frozen foods now that electricity was gone from the city.

For the rest of it, he had to straighten up the garage and clean out the debris of broken bulbs, fuses, wiring, plugs, solder, spare motor parts, and a box of seeds he'd put there once; he didn't remember just when.

The washing machine they had ruined beyond repair, forcing him to replace it. But that wasn't hard. The worst part was mopping up all the gasoline they'd spilled from the drums. They'd really outdone themselves spilling gasoline, he thought irritably while he mopped it up.

Inside the house, he had repaired the cracked plaster, and as an added fillip he had put up another wall mural to give a different appearance to the room.

He'd almost enjoyed all the work once it was started. It gave him something to lose himself in, something to pour all the energy of his still pulsing fury into. It broke the monotony of his daily tasks: the carrying away of bodies, the repairing of the house's exterior, the hanging of garlic.

He drank sparingly during those days, managing to pass almost the entire day without a drink, even allowing his evening drinks to assume the function of relaxing nightcaps rather than senseless escape. His appetite increased and he gained four pounds and lost a little belly. He even slept nights, a tired sleep without the dreams.

For a day or so he had played with the idea of moving to some lavish hotel suite. But the thought of all the work he'd have to do to make it habitable changed his mind. No, he was all set in the house.

Now he sat in the living room, listening to Mozart's Jupiter Symphony and wondering how he was to begin, *where* he was to begin his investigation.

He knew a few details, but these were only landmarks above

the basic earth of cause. The answer lay in something else. Probably in some fact he was aware of but did not adequately appreciate, in some apparent knowledge he had not yet connected with the overall picture.

But what?

He sat motionless in the chair, a sweat-beaded glass in his right hand, his eyes fastened on the mural.

It was a scene from Canada: deep northern woods, mysterious with green shadows, standing aloof and motionless, heavy with the silence of manless nature. He stared into its soundless green depths and wondered.

Maybe if he went back. Maybe the answer lay in the past, in some obscure crevice of memory. Go back, then, he told his mind, go back.

It tore his heart out to go back.

There had been another dust storm during the night. High, spinning winds had scoured the house with grit, driven it through the cracks, sifted it through plaster pores, and left a hair-thin layer of dust across all the furniture surfaces. Over their bed the dust filtered like fine powder, settling in their hair and on their eyelids and under their nails, clogging their pores.

Half the night he'd lain awake trying to single out the sound of Virginia's labored breathing. But he couldn't hear anything above the shrieking, grating sound of the storm. For a while, in the suspension between sleeping and waking, he had suffered the illusion that the house was being sandpapered by giant wheels that held its framework between monstrous abrasive surfaces and made it shudder.

He'd never got used to the dust storms. That hissing sound of whirlwind granulation always set his teeth on edge. The storms had never come regularly enough to allow him to adapt himself to them. Whenever they came, he spent a restless, tossing night, and went to the plant the next day with jaded mind and body.

Now there was Virginia to worry about too.

About four o'clock he awoke from a thin depression of sleep and realized that the storm had ended. The contrast made silence a rushing noise in his ears.

As he raised his body irritably to adjust his twisted pajamas, he noticed that Virginia was awake. She was lying on her back and staring at the ceiling.

'What's the matter?' he mumbled drowsily.

She didn't answer.

'Honey?'

Her eyes moved slowly to him.

'Nothing,' she said. 'Go to sleep.'

'How do you feel?'

'The same.'

'Oh.'

He lay there for a moment looking at her.

'Well,' he said then and, turning on his side, closed his eyes.

The alarm went off at six-thirty. Usually Virginia pushed in the stop, but when she failed to do so, he reached over her inert body and did it himself. She was still on her back, still staring.

'What is it?' he asked worriedly.

She looked at him and shook her head on the pillow.

'I don't know,' she said. 'I just can't sleep.'

'Why?'

She made an indecisive sound.

'Still feel weak?' he asked.

She tried to sit up but she couldn't.

'Stay there, hon,' he said. 'Don't move.' He put his hand on her brow. 'You haven't got any fever,' he told her.

'I don't feel sick,' she said. 'Just . . . tired.'

'You look pale.'

'I know. I look like a ghost.'

'Don't get up,' he said.

She was up.

'I'm not going to pamper myself,' she said. 'Go ahead, get dressed. I'll be all right.'

'Don't get up if you don't feel good, honey.'

40

She patted his arm and smiled.

'I'll be all right,' she said. 'You get ready.'

While he shaved he heard the shuffling of her slippers past the bathroom door. He opened the door and watched her crossing the living room very slowly, her wrappered body weaving a little. He went back in the bathroom shaking his head. She should have stayed in bed.

The whole top of the washbasin was grimy with dust. The damn stuff was everywhere. He'd finally been compelled to erect a tent over Kathy's bed to keep the dust from her face. He'd nailed one edge of a shelter half to the wall next to her bed and let it slope over the bed, the other edge held up by two poles lashed to the side of the bed.

He didn't get a good shave because there was grit in the shaving soap and he didn't have time for a second lathering. He washed off his face, got a clean towel from the hall closet, and dried himself.

Before going to the bedroom to get dressed he checked Kathy's room.

She was still asleep, her small blonde head motionless on the pillow, her cheeks pink with heavy sleep. He ran a finger across the top of the shelter half and drew it away gray with dust. With a disgusted shake of his head he left the room.

'I wish these damn storms would end,' he said as he entered the kitchen ten minutes later. 'I'm sure . . .'

He stopped talking. Usually she was at the stove turning eggs or French toast or pancakes, making coffee. Today she was sitting at the table. On the stove coffee was percolating, but nothing else was cooking.

'Sweetheart, if you don't feel well, go back to bed,' he told her. 'I can fix my own breakfast.'

'It's all right,' she said. 'I was just resting. I'm sorry. I'll get up and fry you some eggs.'

'Stay there,' he said. 'I'm not helpless.'

He went to the refrigerator and opened the door.

'I'd like to know what this *is* going around,' she said. 'Half

41

the people on the block have it, and you say that more than half the plant is absent.'

'Maybe it's some kind of virus,' he said.

She shook her head. 'I don't know.'

'Between the storms and the mosquitoes and everyone being sick, life is rapidly becoming a pain,' he said, pouring orange juice out of the bottle. 'And speak of the devil.'

He drew a black speck out of the orange juice in the glass.

'How the hell they get in the refrigerator I'll never know,' he said.

'None for me, Bob,' she said.

'No orange juice?'

'No.'

'Good for you.'

'No, thank you, sweetheart,' she said, trying to smile.

He put back the bottle and sat down across from her with his glass of juice.

'You don't feel any pain?' he said. 'No headache, nothing?'

She shook her head slowly.

'I wish I *did* know what was wrong,' she said.

'You call up Dr Busch today.'

'I will,' she said, starting to get up. He put his hand over hers.

'No, no, sweetheart, stay there,' he said.

'But there's no *reason* why I should be like this.'

She sounded angry. That was the way she'd been as long as he'd known her. If she became ill, it irritated her. She was annoyed by sickness. She seemed to regard it as a personal affront.

'Come on,' he said, starting to get up. 'I'll help you back to bed.'

'No, just let me sit here with you,' she said. 'I'll go back to bed after Kathy goes to school.'

'All right. Don't you want something, though?'

'No.'

'How about coffee?'

She shook her head.

'You're *really* going to get sick if you don't eat,' he said.

'I'm just not hungry.'

He finished his juice and got up to fry a couple of eggs. He cracked them on the side of the iron skillet and dropped the contents into the melted bacon fat. He got the bread from the drawer and went over to the table with it.

'Here, I'll put it in the toaster,' Virginia said. 'You watch your . . . Oh, God.'

'What is it?'

She waved one hand weakly in front of her face.

'A mosquito,' she said with a grimace.

He moved over and, after a moment, crushed it between his two palms.

'Mosquitoes,' she said. 'Flies, sand fleas.'

'We are entering the age of the insect,' he said.

'It's not good,' she said. 'They carry diseases. We ought to put a net around Kathy's bed too.'

'I know, I know,' he said, returning to the stove and tipping the skillet so the hot fat ran over the white egg surfaces. 'I keep meaning to.'

'I don't think that spray works, either,' Virginia said.

'It doesn't?'

'No.'

'My God, and it's supposed to be one of the best ones on the market.'

He slid the eggs onto a dish.

'Sure you don't want some coffee?' he asked her.

'No, thank you.'

He sat down and she handed him the buttered toast.

'I hope to hell we're not breeding a race of super-bugs,' he said. 'You remember that strain of giant grasshoppers they found in Colorado?'

'Yes.'

'Maybe the insects are . . . What's the word? Mutating.'

'What's that?'

43

'Oh, it means they're . . . changing. Suddenly. Jumping over dozens of small evolutionary steps, maybe developing along lines they might not have followed at all if it weren't for . . .'

Silence.

'The bombings?' she said.

'Maybe,' he said.

'Well, they're causing the dust storms. They're probably causing a lot of things.'

She sighed wearily and shook her head.

'And they say we won the war,' she said.

'Nobody won it.'

'The mosquitoes won it.'

He smiled a little.

'I guess they did,' he said.

They sat there for a few moments without talking and the only sound in the kitchen was the clink of his fork on the plate and the cup on the saucer.

'You looked at Kathy last night?' she asked.

'I just looked at her now. She looks fine.'

'Good.'

She looked at him studiedly.

'I've been thinking, Bob,' she said. 'Maybe we should send her East to your mother's until I get better. It may be contagious.'

'We could,' he said dubiously, 'but if it's contagious, my mother's place wouldn't be any safer than here.'

'You don't think so?' she asked. She looked worried.

He shrugged. 'I don't know, hon. I think probably she's just as safe here. If it starts to get bad on the block, we'll keep her out of school.'

She started to say something, then stopped.

'All right,' she said.

He looked at his watch.

'I'd better finish up,' he said.

She nodded and he ate the rest of his breakfast quickly.

While he was draining the coffee cup she asked him if he'd bought a paper the night before.

'It's in the living room,' he told her.

'Anything new in it?'

'No. Same old stuff. It's all over the country, a little here, a little there. They haven't been able to find the germ yet.'

She bit her lower lip.

'Nobody knows what it is?'

'I doubt it. If anybody did they'd have surely said so by now.'

'But they must have *some* idea.'

'Everybody's got an idea. But they aren't worth anything.'

'What do they say?'

He shrugged. 'Everything from germ warfare on down.'

'Do you think it is?'

'Germ warfare?'

'Yes,' she said.

'The war's over,' he said.

'Bob,' she said suddenly, 'do you think you should go to work?'

He smiled helplessly.

'What else can I do?' he asked. 'We have to eat.'

'I know, but . . .'

He reached across the table and felt how cold her hand was.

'Honey, it'll be all right,' he said.

'And you think I should send Kathy to school?'

'I think so,' he said. 'Unless the health authorities say schools have to shut down, I don't see why we should keep her home. She's not sick.'

'But all the kids at school.'

'I think we'd better, though,' he said.

She made a tiny sound in her throat. Then she said, 'All right. If you think so.'

'Is there anything you want before I go?' he asked.

She shook her head.

'Now you stay in the house today,' he told her, 'and in bed.'

45

'I will,' she said. 'As soon as I send Kathy off.'

He patted her hand. Outside, the car horn sounded. He finished the coffee and went to the bathroom to rinse out his mouth. Then he got his jacket from the hall closet and pulled it on.

'Good-by, honey,' he said, kissing her on the cheek. 'Take it easy, now.'

'Good-by,' she said. 'Be careful.'

He moved across the lawn, gritting his teeth at the residue of dust in the air. He could smell it as he walked, a dry tickling sensation in his nasal passages.

'Morning,' he said, getting in the car and pulling the door shut behind him.

'Good morning,' said Ben Cortman.

CHAPTER SEVEN

'Distilled from *Allium sativum*, genus of Liliaceae comprising garlic, leek, onion, shallot, and chive. Is of pale color and penetrating odor, containing several allyl sulphides. Composition: water, 64.6%; protein, 6.8%; fat, 0.1%; carbohydrates, 26.3%; fiber, 0.8%; ash 1.4%.'

There it was. He jiggled one of the pink, leathery cloves in his right palm. For seven months now he'd strung them together into aromatic necklaces and hung them outside his house without the remotest idea of why they chased the vampires away. It was time he learned why.

He put the clove on the sink ledge. Leek, onion, shallot, and chive. Would they all work as well as garlic? He'd really feel like a fool if they did, after searching miles around for garlic when onions were everywhere.

He mashed the clove to a pulp and smelled the acrid fluid on the thick cleaver blade.

All right, what now? The past revealed nothing to help him; only talk of insect carriers and virus, and they weren't the causes. He was sure of it.

The past had brought something else, though; pain at remembering. Every recalled word had been like a knife blade twisting in him. Old wounds had been reopened with every thought of her. He'd finally had to stop, eyes closed, fists clenched, trying desperately to accept the present on its own terms and not yearn with his very flesh for the past. But only enough drinks to stultify all introspection had managed to drive away the enervating sorrow that remembering brought.

He focused his eyes. All right, damn it, he told himself, *do* something!

He looked at the text again, water – was it that? he asked himself. No, that was ridiculous; all things had water in them. Protein? No. Fat? No. Carbohydrates? No. Fiber? No. Ash? No. What then?

'The characteristic odor and flavor of garlic are due to an essential oil amounting to about 0.2% of the weight, which consists mainly of allyl sulphide and allyl isothicyanate.'

Maybe the answer was there.

Again the book: 'Allyl sulphide may be prepared by heating mustard oil and potassium sulphide at 100 degrees.'

His body thudded down into the living-room chair and a disgusted breath shuddered his long frame. And where the hell do I get mustard oil and potassium sulphide? *And* the equipment to prepare them in?

That's great, he railed at himself. The first step, and already you've fallen flat on your face.

He pushed himself up disgustedly and headed for the bar. But halfway through pouring a drink he slammed down the bottle. No, by God, he had no intention of going on like a blind man, plodding down a path of brainless, fruitless existence until old age or accident took him. Either he found the answer or he ditched the whole mess, life included.

He checked his watch. Ten-twenty A.M.; still time. He moved to the hallway resolutely and checked through the telephone directories. There was a place in Inglewood.

Four hours later he straightened up from the workbench with a crick in his neck and the allyl sulphide inside a hypodermic syringe, and in himself the first sense of real accomplishment since his forced isolation began. A little excited, he ran to his car and drove out past the area he'd cleared out and marked with chalked rods. He knew it was more than possible that some vampires might have wandered

48

into the cleared area and were hiding there again. But he had no time for searching.

Parking his car, he went into a house and walked to the bedroom. A young woman lay there, a coating of blood on her mouth.

Flipping her over, Neville pulled up her skirt and injected the allyl sulphide into her soft, fleshy buttock, then turned her over again and stepped back. For a half hour he stood there watching her.

Nothing happened.

This doesn't make sense, his mind argued. I hang garlic around the house and the vampires stay away. And the characteristic of garlic is the oil I've injected in her. But nothing's happened.

Goddamn it, nothing's happened!

He flung down the syringe and, trembling with rage and frustration, went home again. Before darkness, he built a small wooden structure on the front lawn and hung strings of onions on it. He spent a listless night, only the knowledge that there was still much left to do keeping him from the liquor.

In the morning he went out and looked at the matchwood on his lawn.

The cross. He held one in his hand, gold and shiny in the morning sun. This, too, drove the vampires away.

Why? Was there a logical answer, something he could accept without slipping on banana skins of mysticism?

There was only one way to find out.

He took the woman from her bed, pretending not to notice the question posed in his mind: Why do you always experiment on women? He didn't care to admit that the inference had any validity. She just happened to be the first one he'd come across, that was all. What about the man in the living room, though? For God's sake! he flared back. I'm not going to rape the woman!

Crossing your fingers, Neville? Knocking on wood?

49

He ignored that, beginning to suspect his mind of harboring an alien. Once he might have termed it conscience. Now it was only an annoyance. Morality, after all, had fallen with society. He was his own ethic.

Makes a good excuse, doesn't it, Neville? Oh, shut up.

But he wouldn't let himself pass the afternoon near her. After binding her to a chair, he secluded himself in the garage and puttered around with the car. She was wearing a torn black dress and too much was visible as she breathed. Out of sight, out of mind. . . . It was a lie, he knew, but he wouldn't admit it.

At last, mercifully, night came. He locked the garage door, went back to the house, and locked the front door, putting the heavy bar across it. Then he made a drink and sat down on the couch across from the woman.

From the ceiling, right before her face, hung the cross.

At six-thirty her eyes opened. Suddenly, like the eyes of a sleeper who has a definite job to do upon awakening; who does not move into consciousness with a vague entry, but with a single, clearcut motion, knowing just what is to be done.

Then she saw the cross and she jerked her eyes from it with a sudden rattling gasp and her body twisted in the chair.

'Why are you afraid of it?' he asked, startled at the sound of his own voice after so long.

Her eyes, suddenly on him, made him shudder. The way they glowed, the way her tongue licked across her red lips as if it were a separate life in her mouth. The way she flexed her body as if trying to move it closer to him. A guttural rumbling filled her throat like the sound of a dog defending its bone.

'The cross,' he said nervously. 'Why are you afraid of it?'

She strained against her bonds, her hands raking across the sides of the chair. No words from her, only a harsh, gasping succession of breaths. Her body writhed on the chair, her eyes burned into him.

'The cross!' he snapped angrily.

He was on his feet, the glass falling and splashing across the

50

rug. He grabbed the string with tense fingers and swung the cross before her eyes. She flung her head away with a frightened snarl and recoiled into the chair.

'*Look* at it!' he yelled at her.

A sound of terror-stricken whining came from her. Her eyes moved wildly around the room, great white eyes with pupils like specks of soot.

He grabbed at her shoulder, then jerked his hand back. It was dribbling blood from raw teeth wounds.

His stomach muscles jerked in. The hand lashed out again, this time smashing her across the cheek and snapping her head to the side.

Ten minutes later he threw her body out the front door and slammed it again in their faces. Then he stood there against the door breathing heavily. Faintly he heard through the sound-proofing the sound of them fighting like jackals for the spoils.

Later he went to the bathroom and poured alcohol into the teeth gouges, enjoying fiercely the burning pain in his flesh.

CHAPTER EIGHT

Neville bent over and picked up a little soil in his right hand. He ran it between his fingers, crumbling the dark lumps into grit How many of them, he wondered, slept in the soil, as the story went?

He shook his head. Precious few.

Where did the legend fit in, then?

He closed his eyes and let the dirt filter down slowly from his hand. Was there any answer? If only he could remember whether those who slept in soil were the ones who had returned from death. He might have theorized then.

But he couldn't remember. Another unanswerable question, then. Add it to the question that had occurred to him the night before.

What would a Mohammedan vampire do if faced with a cross?

The barking sound of his laugh in the silent morning air startled him. Good God, he thought, it's been so long since I've laughed, I've forgotten how. It sounded like the cough of a sick hound. Well, that's what I am, after all, isn't it? he decided. A very sick dog.

There had been a light dust storm about four that morning. Strange how it brought back memories. Virginia, Kathy, all those horrible days . . .

He caught himself. No, *no*, there was danger there. It was thinking of the past that drove him to the bottle. He was just going to have to accept the present.

He found himself wondering again why he chose to go on living. Probably, he thought, there's no real reason. I'm just too dumb to end it all.

Well – he clapped his hands with false decision – what now? He looked around as if there were something to see along the stillness of Cimarron Street.

All right, he decided impulsively, let's see if the running-water bit makes sense.

He buried a hose under the ground and ran it into a small trough constructed of wood. The water ran through the trough and out another hole into more hosing, which conducted the water into the earth.

When he'd finished, he went in and took a shower, shaved, and took the bandage off his hand. The wound had healed cleanly. But then, he hadn't been overly concerned about that. Time had more than proved to him that he was immune to their infection.

At six-twenty he went into the living room and stood before the peephole. He stretched a little, grunting at the ache in his muscles. Then, when nothing happened, he made himself a drink.

When he got back to the peephole, he saw Ben Cortman come walking onto the lawn.

'Come out, Neville,' Robert Neville muttered, and Cortman echoed the words in a loud cry.

Neville stood there motionless, looking at Ben Cortman.

Ben hadn't changed much. His hair was still black, his body inclined to corpulence, his face still white. But there was a beard on his face now; mostly under the nose, thinner around his chin and cheeks and under his throat. That was the only real difference, though. Ben had always been immaculately shaved in the old days, smelling of cologne each morning when he picked up Neville to drive to the plant.

It was strange to stand there looking out at Ben Cortman; a Ben completely alien to him now. Once he had spoken to that man, ridden to work with him, talked about cars and baseball and politics with him, later on about the disease, about how Virginia and Kathy were getting along, about how Freda Cortman was, about . . .

Neville shook his head. There was no point going into that. The past was as dead as Cortman.

Again he shook his head. The world's gone mad, he thought. The dead walk about and I think nothing of it. The return of corpses has become trivial in import. How quickly one accepts the incredible if only one sees it enough!

Neville stood there, sipping his whisky and wondering who it was that Ben reminded him of. He'd felt for some time that Cortman reminded him of somebody, but for the life of him he couldn't think who.

He shrugged. What was the difference?

He put down the glass on the window sill and went into the kitchen. He turned on the water there and went back in. When he reached the peephole, he saw another man and a woman on the lawn. None of the three was speaking to either of the others. They never did. They walked and walked about on restless feet, circling each other like wolves, never looking at each other once, having hungry eyes only for the house and their prey inside the house.

Then Cortman saw the water running through the trough and went over to look at it. After a moment he lifted his white face and Neville saw him grinning.

Neville stiffened.

Cortman was jumping over the trough, then back again. Neville felt his throat tightening. The bastard knew!

With rigid legs he pistoned himself into the bedroom and, with shaking hands, pulled one of his pistols out of the bureau drawer.

Cortman was just about finishing stamping in the sides of the trough when the bullet struck him in the left shoulder.

He staggered back with a grunt and flopped onto the sidewalk with a kicking of legs. Neville fired again and the bullet whined up off the cement, inches from Cortman's twisting body.

Cortman started up with a snarl and the third bullet struck him full in the chest.

Neville stood there watching, smelling the acrid fumes of the pistol smoke. Then the woman blocked his view of Cortman and started jerking up her dress.

Neville pulled back and slammed the tiny door over the peephole. He wasn't going to let himself look at that. In the first second of it, he had felt that terrible heat dredging up from his loins like something ravenous.

Later he looked out again and saw Ben Cortman pacing around, calling for him to come out.

And, in the moonlight, he suddenly realized who Cortman reminded him of. The idea made his chest shudder with repressed laughter and he turned away as the shaking reached his shoulders.

My God – *Oliver Hardy*! Those old two-reelers he'd looked at with his projector. Cortman was almost a dead ringer for the roly-poly comedian. A little less plump, that was all. Even the mustache was there now.

Oliver Hardy flopping on his back under the driving impact of bullets. Oliver Hardy always coming back for more, no matter what happened. Ripped by bullets, punctured by knives, flattened by cars, smashed under collapsing chimneys and boats, submerged in water, flung through pipes. And always returning, patient and bruised. That was who Ben Cortman was – a hideously malignant Oliver Hardy buffeted and long-suffering.

My God, it was hilarious!

He couldn't stop laughing because it was more than laughter; it was release. Tears flooded down his cheeks. The glass in his hand shook so badly, the liquor spilled all over him and made him laugh harder. Then the glass fell thumping on the rug as his body jerked with spasms of uncontrollable amusement and the room was filled with his gasping, nerve-shattered laughter.

Later, he cried.

He drove it into the stomach, into the shoulder. Into the neck with a single mallet blow. Into the legs and the arms, and always the same result: the blood pulsing out, slick and crimson, over the white flesh.

He thought he'd found the answer. It was a matter of losing the blood they lived by; it was hemorrhage.

But then he found the woman in the small green and white house, and when he drove in the stake, the dissolution was so sudden it made him lurch away and lose his breakfast.

When he had recovered enough to look again, he saw on the bedspread what looked like a row of salt and pepper mixed; just about as long as the woman had been. It was the first time he'd ever seen such a thing.

Shaken by the sight, he went out of the house on trembling legs and sat in the car for an hour, drinking the flask empty. But even liquor couldn't drive away the vision.

It had been so *quick*. With the sound of the mallet blow still in his ears, she had virtually dissolved before his eyes.

He recalled talking once to a Negro at the plant. The man had studied mortuary science and had told Robert Neville about the mausoleums where people were stored in vacuum drawers and never changed their appearance.

'But you just let some air in,' the Negro had said, 'and *whoom*! – they'll look like a row of salt and pepper. Jus' like *that*!' And he snapped his fingers.

The woman had been long dead, then. Maybe, the thought occurred, she was one of the vampires who had originally started the plague. God only knew how many years she'd been cheating death.

He was too unnerved to do any more that day or for days to come. He stayed home and drank to forget and let the bodies

56

pile up on the lawn and let the outside of the house fall into disrepair.

For days he sat in the chair with his liquor and thought about the woman. And, no matter how hard he tried not to, no matter how much he drank, he kept thinking about Virginia. He kept seeing himself entering the crypt, lifting the coffin lid.

He thought he was coming down with something, so palsied and nerveless was his shivering, so cold and ill did he feel.

Is *that* what she looked like?

CHAPTER NINE

Morning. A sun-bright hush broken only by the chorus of birds in the trees. No breeze to stir the vivid blossoms around the houses, the bushes, the dark-leaved hedges. A cloud of silent heat was suspended over everything on Cimarron Street.

Virginia Neville's heart had stopped.

He sat beside her on the bed, looking down at her white face. He held her fingers in his hand, his fingertips stroking and stroking. His body was immobile, one rigid, insensible block of flesh and bone. His eyes did not blink, his mouth was a static line, and the movement of his breathing was so slight that it seemed to have stopped altogether.

Something had happened to his brain.

In the second he had felt no heartbeat beneath his trembling fingers, the core of his brain seemed to have petrified, sending out jagged lines of calcification until his head felt like stone. Slowly, on palsied legs, he had sunk down on the bed. And now, vaguely, deep in the struggling tissues of thought, he did not understand how he could sit there, did not understand why despair did not crush him to the earth. But prostration would not come. Time was caught on hooks and could not progress. Everything stood fixed. With Virginia, life and the world had shuddered to a halt.

Thirty minutes passed; forty.

Then, slowly, as though he were discovering some objective phenomenon, he found his body trembling. Not with a local-ized tremble, a nerve here, a muscle there. This was complete.

His body shuddered without end, one mass entire of nerves without control, bereft of will. And what operative mind was left knew that this was his reaction.

For more than an hour he sat in this palsied state, his eyes fastened dumbly to her face.

Then, abruptly, it ended, and with a choked muttering in his throat he lurched up from the bed and left the room.

Half the whisky splashed on the sink top as he poured. The liquor that managed to reach the glass he bolted down in a swallow. The thin current flared its way down to his stomach, feeling twice as intense in the polar numbness of his flesh. He stood sagged against the sink. Hands shaking, he filled the glass again to its top and gulped the burning whisky down with great convulsive swallows.

It's a dream, he argued vainly. It was as if a voice spoke the words aloud in his head.

'Virginia . . .'

He kept turning from one side to another, his eyes searching around the room as if there were something to be found, as if he had mislaid the exit from this house of horror. Tiny sounds of disbelief pulsed in his throat. He pressed his hands together, forcing the shaking palms against each other, the twitching fingers intertwining confusedly.

His hands began to shake so he couldn't make out their forms. With a gagging intake of breath he jerked them apart and pressed them against his legs.

'*Virginia.*'

He took a step and cried aloud as the room flung itself off balance. Pain exploded in his right knee, sending hot barbs up his leg. He whined as he pushed himself up and stumbled to the living room. He stood there like a statue in an earthquake, his marble eyes frozen on the bedroom door.

In his mind he saw a scene enacted once again.

The great fire crackling, roaring yellow, sending its dense and grease-thick clouds into the sky. Kathy's tiny body in his arms. The man coming up and snatching her away as if he

59

were taking a bundle of rags. The man lunging into the dark mist carrying his baby. Him standing there while pile-driver blows of horror drove him down with their impact.

Then suddenly he had darted forward with a berserk scream.

'Kathy!'

The arms caught him, the men in canvas and masks drawing him back. His shoes gouged frenziedly at the earth, digging two ragged trenches in the earth as they dragged him away. His brain exploded, the terrified screams flooding from him.

Then the sudden bolt of numbing pain in his jaw, the daylight swept over with clouds of night. The hot trickle of liquor down his throat, the coughing, a gasping, and then he had been sitting silent and rigid in Ben Cortman's car, staring as they drove away at the gigantic pall of smoke that rose above the earth like a black wraith of all earth's despair.

Remembering, he closed his eyes suddenly and his teeth pressed together until they ached.

'*No.*'

He wouldn't put Virginia there. Not if they killed him for it.

With a slow, stiff motion he walked to the front door and went out on the porch. Stepping off onto the yellowing lawn, he started down the block for Ben Cortman's house. The glare of the sun made his pupils shrink to points of jet. His hands swung useless and numbed at his sides.

The chimes still played 'How Dry I Am.' The absurdity of it made him want to break something in his hands. He remembered when Ben had put them in, thinking how funny it would be.

He stood rigidly before the door, his mind still pulsing. I don't care if it's the law, I don't care if refusal means death, I won't put her there!

His fist thudded on the door.

'*Ben!*'

Silence in the house of Ben Cortman. White curtains hung motionless in the front windows. He could see the red couch, the floor lamp with the fringed shade, the upright Knabe Freda used to toy with on Sunday afternoons. He blinked. What day *was* it? He had forgotten, he had lost track of the days.

He twisted his shoulders as impatient fury hosed acids through his veins.

'*Ben!*'

Again the side of his hard fist pummeled the door, and the flesh along his whitening jawline twitched. Damn him, where *was* he? Neville jammed in the button with a brittle finger and the chimes started the tippler's song over and over and over. 'How dry I am, how dry I am, how dry I am, how dry I . . .'

With a frenzied gasp he lurched against the door and it flew open against the inside wall. It had been unlocked.

He walked into the silent living room.

'Ben,' he said loudly. 'Ben, I need your car.'

They were in the bedroom, silent and still in their daytime comas, lying apart on the twin beds, Ben in pajamas, Freda in silk nightgown; lying on the sheets, their thick chests faltering with labored breath.

He stood there for a moment looking down at them. There were some wounds on Freda's white neck that had crusted over with dried blood. His eyes moved to Ben. There was no wound on Ben's throat. And he heard a voice in his mind that said: If only I'd wake up.

He shook his head. No, there was no waking up from this.

He found the car keys on the bureau and picked them up. He turned away and left the silent house behind. It was the last time he ever saw either of them alive.

The motor coughed into life and he let it idle a few minutes, choke out, while he sat staring out through the dusty windshield. A fly buzzed its bloated form around his head in the hot, airless interior of the car. He watched the dull green glitter of it and felt the car pulsing under him.

After a moment he pushed in the choke and drove the car up the street. He parked it in the driveway before his garage and turned off the motor.

The house was cool and silent. His shoes scuffed quietly over the rug, then clicked on the floor boards in the hall.

He stood motionless in the doorway looking at her. She still lay on her back, arms at her sides, the white fingers slightly curled in. She looked as if she were sleeping.

He turned away and went back into the living room. What was he going to do? Choices seemed pointless now. What did it matter *what* he did? Life would be equally purposeless no matter what his decision was.

He stood before the window looking out at the quiet, sun-drenched street, his eyes lifeless.

Why did I get the car, then? he wondered. His throat moved as he swallowed. I can't burn her, he thought. I *won't*. But what else was there? Funeral parlors were closed. What few morticians were healthy enough to practice were prevented from doing so by law. Everyone without exception had to be transported to the fires immediately upon death. It was the only way they knew now to prevent communication. Only flames could destroy the bacteria that caused the plague.

He knew that. He knew it was the law. But how many people followed it? He wondered that too. How many husbands took the women who had shared their life and love and dropped them into flames? How many parents incinerated the children they adored, how many children tossed their beloved parents on a bonfire a hundred yards square, a hundred feet deep?

No, if there was anything left in the world, it was his vow that she would not be burned in the fire.

An hour passed before he finally reached a decision.

Then he went and got her needle and thread.

He kept sewing until only her face showed. Then, fingers trembling, a tight knot in his stomach, he sewed the blanket together over her mouth. Over her nose. Her eyes.

Finished, he went in the kitchen and drank another glass of whisky. It didn't seem to affect him at all.

At last he went back to the bedroom on faltering legs. For a long minute he stood there breathing hoarsely. Then he bent over and worked his arms under her inert form.

'Come on, baby,' he whispered.

The words seemed to loosen everything. He felt himself shaking, felt the tears running slowly down his cheeks as he carried her through the living room and outside.

He put her in the back seat and got in the car. He took a deep breath and reached for the starter button.

He drew back. Getting out of the car again, he went into the garage and got the shovel.

He twitched as he came out, seeing the man across the street approaching slowly. He put the shovel in the back and got in the car.

'Wait!'

The man's shout was hoarse. The man tried to run, but he wasn't strong enough.

Robert Neville sat there silently as the man came shuffling up.

'Could you . . . let me bring my . . . my mother too?' the man said stiffly.

'I . . . I . . . I . . .'

Neville's brain wouldn't function. He thought he was going to cry again, but he caught himself and stiffened his back.

'I'm not going to the . . . *there*,' he said.

The man looked at him blankly.

'But your . . .'

'I'm not going to the fire, I said!' Neville blurted out, and jabbed in the starter button.

'But your wife,' said the man. 'You have your . . .'

Robert Neville jerked the gear shift into reverse.

'*Please*,' begged the man.

'I'm not *going* there!' Neville shouted without looking at the man.

'But it's the *law*!' the man shouted back, suddenly furious.

The car raced back quickly into the street and Neville jerked it around to face Compton Boulevard. As he sped away he saw the man standing at the curb watching him leave. Fool! his mind grated. Do you think I'm going to throw my wife into a fire?

The streets were deserted. He turned left at Compton and started west. As he drove he looked at the huge lot on the right side of the car. He couldn't use any of the cemeteries. They were locked and watched. Men had been shot trying to bury their loved ones.

He turned right at the next block and drove up one block, turned right again into a quiet street that ended in the lot. Halfway up the block he cut the motor. He rolled the rest of the way so no one would hear the car.

No one saw him carry her from the car or carry her deep into the high-weeded lot. No one saw him put her down on an open patch of ground and then disappear from view as he knelt.

Slowly he dug, pushing the shovel into the soft earth, the bright sun pouring heat into the little clearing like molten air into a dish. Sweat ran in many lines down his cheeks and forehead as he dug, and the earth swam dizzily before his eyes. Newly thrown dirt filled his nostrils with its hot, pungent smell.

At last the hole was finished. He put down the shovel and sagged down on his knees. His body shuddered and sweat trickled over his face. This was the part he dreaded.

But he knew he couldn't wait. If he was seen they would come out and get him. Being shot was nothing. But she would be burned then. His lips tightened. No.

Gently, as carefully as he could, he lowered her into the shallow grave, making sure that her head did not bump.

He straightened up and looked down at her still body sewn up in the blanket. For the last time, he thought. No more talking, no more loving. Eleven wonderful years ending in a filled-in trench. He began to tremble. No, he ordered himself, there's no time for that.

It was no use. The world shimmered through endless

distorting tears while he pressed back the hot earth, patting it around her still body with nerveless fingers.

He lay fully clothed on his bed, staring at the black ceiling. He was half drunk and the darkness spun with fireflies.

His right arm faltered out for the table. His hand brushed the bottle over and he jerked out clawing fingers too late. Then he relaxed and lay there in the still of night, listening to the whisky gurgle out of the bottle mouth and spread across the floor.

His unkempt hair rustled on the pillow as he looked toward the clock. Two in the morning. Two days since he'd buried her. Two eyes looking at the clock, two ears picking up the hum of its electric chronology, two lips pressed together, two hands lying on the bed.

He tried to rid himself of the concept, but everything in the world seemed suddenly to have dropped into a pit of duality, victim to a system of twos. Two people dead, two beds in the room, two windows, two bureaus, two rugs, two hearts that . . .

His chest filled with night air, held, then pushed it out and sank abruptly. Two days, two hands, two eyes, two legs, two feet . . .

He sat up and dropped his legs over the edge of the bed. His feet landed in the puddle of whisky and he felt it soaking through his socks. A cold breeze was rattling the window blinds.

He stared at the blackness. What's left? he asked himself. What's left, anyway?

Wearily he stood up and stumbled into the bathroom, leaving wet tracks behind him. He threw water into his face and fumbled for a towel.

What's left? What's . . .

He stood suddenly rigid in the cold blackness.

Someone was turning the knob on the front door.

He felt a chill move up the back of his neck and his scalp

began prickling. It's Ben, he heard his mind offering. He's come for the car keys.

The towel slipped from his fingers and he heard it swish down onto the tiles. His body twitched.

A fist thudded against the door; strengthless, as if it had fallen against the wood.

He moved into the living room slowly, his heartbeat thudding heavily.

The door rattled as another fist thudded against it weakly. He felt himself twitch at the sound. What's the matter? he thought. The door is open. From the open window a cold breeze blew across his face. The darkness drew him to the door.

'Who . . .' he murmured, unable to go on.

His hand recoiled from the doorknob as it turned under his fingers. With one step, he backed into the wall and stood there breathing harshly, his widened eyes staring.

Nothing happened. He stood there holding himself rigidly.

Then his breath was snuffed. Someone was mumbling on the porch, muttering words he couldn't hear. He braced himself; then, with a lunge, he jerked open the door and let the moonlight in.

He couldn't even scream. He just stood rooted to the spot, staring dumbly at Virginia.

'Rob . . . ert,' she said.

CHAPTER TEN

The science room was on the second floor. Robert Neville's footsteps thudded hollowly up the marble steps of the Los Angeles Public Library. It was April 7, 1976.

It had come to him, after a half week of drinking, disgust, and desultory investigation, that he was wasting his time. Isolated experiments were yielding nothing, that was clear. If there was a rational answer to the problem (and he had to believe that there was), he could only find it by careful research.

Tentatively, for want of better knowledge, he had set up a possible basis, and that was blood. It provided, at least, a starting point. Step number one, then, was reading about blood.

The silence of the library was complete save for the thudding of his shoes as he walked along the second-floor hallway. Outside, there were birds sometimes and, even lacking that, there seemed to be a sort of sound outside. Inexplicable, perhaps, but it never seemed as deathly still in the open as it did inside a building.

Especially here in this giant, gray-stoned building that housed the literature of a world's dead. Probably it was being surrounded by walls, he thought, something purely psychological. But knowing that didn't make it any easier. There were no psychiatrists left to murmur of groundless neuroses and auditory hallucinations. The last man in the world was irretrievably stuck with his delusions.

He entered the Science Room.

It was a high-ceilinged room with tall, large-paned windows.

Across from the doorway was the desk where books had been checked out in days when books were still being checked out.

He stood there for a moment looking around the silent room, shaking his head slowly. All these books, he thought, the residue of a planet's intellect, the scrapings of futile minds, the leftovers, the potpourri of artifacts that had no power to save men from perishing.

His shoes clicked across the dark tiles as he walked to the beginning of the shelves on his left. His eyes moved to the cards between shelf sections. 'Astronomy,' he read; books about the heavens. He moved by them. It was not the heavens he was concerned about. Man's lust for the stars had died with the others. 'Physics,' 'Chemistry,' 'Engineering.' He passed them by and entered the main reading section of the Science Room.

He stopped and looked up at the high ceiling. There were two banks of dead lights overhead and the ceiling was divided into great sunken squares, each square decorated with what looked like Indian mosaics. Morning sunlight filtered through the dusty windows and he saw motes floating gently on the current of its beams.

He looked down the row of long wooden tables with chairs lined up before them. Someone had put them in place very neatly. The day the library was shut down, he thought, some maiden librarian had moved down the room, pushing each chair against its table. Carefully, with a plodding precision that was the cachet of herself.

He thought about that visionary lady. To die, he thought, never knowing the fierce joy and attendant comfort of a loved one's embrace. To sink into that hideous coma, to sink then into death and, perhaps, return to sterile, awful wanderings. All without knowing what it was to love and be loved.

That was a tragedy more terrible than becoming a vampire.

He shook his head. All right, that's enough, he told himself, you haven't got the time for maudlin reveries.

He bypassed books until he came to 'Medicine.' That was what he wanted. He looked through the titles. Books on hygiene, on anatomy, on physiology (general and specialized), on curative practices. Farther down, on bacteriology.

He pulled out five books on general physiology and several works on blood. These he stacked on one of the dust-surfaced tables. Should he get any of the books on bacteriology? He stood a minute, looking indecisively at the buckram backs.

Finally he shrugged. Well, what's the difference? he thought. They can't do any harm. He pulled out several of them at random and added them to the pile. He now had nine books on the table. That was enough for a start. He expected he'd be coming back.

As he left the Science Room, he looked up at the clock over the door.

The red hands had stopped at four-twenty-seven. He wondered what day they had stopped. As he descended the stairs with his armful of books, he wondered at just what moment the clock had stopped. Had it been morning or night? Was it raining or shining? Was anyone there when it stopped?

He twisted his shoulders irritably. For God's sake, what's the difference? he asked himself. He was getting disgusted at this increasing nostalgic preoccupation with the past. It was a weakness, he knew, a weakness he could scarcely afford if he intended to go on. And yet he kept discovering himself drifting into extensive meditation on aspects of the past. It was almost more than he could control, and it was making him furious with himself.

He couldn't get the huge front doors open from the inside, either; they were too well locked. He had to go out through the broken window again, first dropping the books to the sidewalk one at a time, then himself. He took the books to his car and got in.

As he started the car, he saw that he was parked along a red-painted curb, facing in the wrong direction on a one-way street. He looked up and down the street.

'Policeman!' he found himself calling. 'Oh, policeman!'

He laughed for a mile without stopping, wondering just what was so funny about it.

He put down the book. He'd been reading again about the lymphatic system. He vaguely remembered reading about it months before, during the time he now called his 'frenzied period.' But what he'd read had made no impression on him then because he'd had nothing to apply it to.

There seemed to be something there now.

The thin walls of the blood capillaries permitted blood plasma to escape into the tissue spaces along with the red and colorless cells. These escaped materials eventually returned to the blood system through the lymphatic vessels, carried back by the thin fluid called lymph.

During this return flow, the lymph trickled through lymph nodes, which interrupted the flow and filtered out the solid particles of body waste, thus preventing them from entering the blood system.

Now.

There were two things that activated the lymphatic system: (1) breathing, which caused the diaphragm to compress the abdominal contents, thus forcing blood and lymph up against gravity; (2) physical movement, which caused skeletal muscles to compress lymph vessels, thus moving the lymph. An intricate valve system prevented any backing up of the flow.

But the vampires didn't breathe; not the dead ones, anyway. That meant, roughly, that *half* of their lymph flow was cut off. This meant, further, that a considerable amount of waste products would be left in the vampire's system.

Robert Neville was thinking particularly of the fetid odor of the vampire.

He read on.

'The bacteria passes into the blood stream, where . . .

'. . . the white corpuscles playing a vital part in our defense against bacterial attack.

'Strong sunlight kills many germs rapidly and . . .

'Many bacterial diseases of man can be disseminated by the mechanical agency of flies, mosquitoes . . .

'. . . where, under the stimulus of bacterial attack, the phagocytic factories rush extra cells into the blood stream.'

He let the book drop forward into his lap and it slipped off his legs and thumped down on the rug.

It was getting harder and harder to fight, because no matter what he read, there was always the relationship between bacteria and blood affliction. Yet, all this time, he'd been letting contempt fall freely on all those in the past who had died proclaiming the truth of the germ theory and scoffing at vampires.

He got up and made himself a drink. But it sat untouched as he stood before the bar. Slowly, rhythmically, he thudded his right fist down on the top of the bar while his eyes stared bleakly at the wall.

Germs.

He grimaced. Well, for God's sake, he snapped jadedly at himself, the word hasn't got thorns, you know.

He took a deep breath. All right, he ordered himself, is there any reason why it couldn't be germs?

He turned away from the bar as if he could leave the question there. But questions had no location; they could follow him around.

He sat in the kitchen staring into a steaming cup of coffee. Germs. Bacteria. Viruses. Vampires. Why am I so against it? he thought. Was it just reactionary stubbornness, or was it that the task would loom as too tremendous for him if it were germs?

He didn't know. He started out on a new course, the course of compromise. Why throw out either theory? One didn't necessarily negate the other. Dual acceptance and correlation, he thought.

Bacteria could be the answer to the vampire.

Everything seemed to flood over him then.

It was as though he'd been the little Dutch boy with his finger in the dike, refusing to let the sea of reason in. There he'd been, crouching and content with his iron-bound theory. Now he'd straightened up and taken his finger out. The sea of answers was already beginning to wash in.

The plague had spread so quickly. Could it have done that if only vampires had spread it? Could their nightly maraudings have propelled it on so quickly?

He felt himself jolted by the sudden answer. Only if you accepted bacteria could you explain the fantastic rapidity of the plague, the geometrical mounting of victims.

He shoved aside the coffee cup, his brain pulsing with a dozen different ideas.

The flies and mosquitoes had been a part of it. Spreading the disease, causing it to race through the world.

Yes, bacteria explained a lot of things; the staying in by day, the coma enforced by the germ to protect itself from sun radiation.

A new idea: What if the bacteria were the strength of the true vampire?

He felt a shudder run down his back. Was it possible that the same germ that killed the living provided the energy for the dead?

He had to know! He jumped up and almost ran out of the house. Then, at the last moment, he jerked back from the door with a nervous laugh. God's *sake*, he thought, am I going out of my mind? It was nighttime.

He grinned and walked restlessly around the living room.

Could it explain the other things? The stake? His mind fell over itself trying to fit that into the framework of bacterial causation. Come on! he shouted impatiently in his mind. But all he could think of was hemorrhage, and that didn't explain that woman. And it wasn't the heart . . .

He skipped it, afraid that his new-found theory would start to collapse before he'd established it.

The cross, then. No, bacteria couldn't explain that. The soil; no, that was no help. Running water, the mirror, garlic . . .

He felt himself trembling without control and he wanted to cry out loudly to stop the runaway horse of his brain. He had to find *something*! Goddamn it! he raged in his mind. I won't let it go!

He made himself sit down. Trembling and rigid, he sat there

and blanked his mind until calm took over. Good Lord, he thought finally, what's the matter with me? I get an idea, and when it doesn't explain everything in the first minute, I panic. I must be going crazy.

He took that drink now; he needed it. He held up his hand until it stopped shaking. All right, little boy, he tried kidding himself, calm down now. Santa Claus is coming to town with all the nice answers. No longer will you be a weird Robinson Crusoe, imprisoned on an island of night surrounded by oceans of death.

He snickered at that, and it relaxed him. Colorful, he thought, tasty. The last man in the world is Edgar Guest.

All right, then, he ordered himself, you're going to bed. You're not going to go flying off in twenty different directions. You can't take that any more; you're an emotional misfit.

The first step was to get a microscope. That is the first step, he kept repeating forcefully to himself as he undressed for bed, ignoring the tight ball of indecision in his stomach, the almost painful craving to plunge directly into investigation without any priming.

He almost felt ill, lying there in the darkness and planning just one step ahead. He knew it had to be that way, though. That is the first step, that is the first step. Goddamn your bones, that is the first step.

He grinned in the darkness, feeling good about the definite work ahead.

One thought on the problem he allowed himself before sleeping. The bitings, the insects, the transmission from person to person – were even these enough to explain the horrible speed with which the plague spread?

He went to sleep with the question in his mind. And, about three in the morning, he woke up to find the house buffeted by another dust storm. And suddenly, in the flash of a second, he made the connection.

CHAPTER ELEVEN

The first one he got was worthless.

The base was so poorly leveled that any vibration at all disturbed it. The action of its moving parts was loose to the point of wobbling. The mirror kept moving out of position because its pivots weren't tight enough. Moreover, the instrument had no substage to hold condenser or polarizer. It had only one nosepiece, so that he had to remove the object lens when he wanted any variation in magnification. The lenses were impossible.

But, of course, he knew nothing about microscopes, and he'd taken the first one he'd found. Three days later he hurled it against the wall with a strangled curse and stamped it into pieces with his heels.

Then, when he'd calmed down, he went to the library and got a book on microscopes.

The next time he went out, he didn't come back until he'd found a decent instrument; triple nose stage, substage for condenser and polarizer, good base, smooth movement, iris diaphragm, good lenses. It's just one more example, he told himself, of the stupidity of starting off half-cocked. Yeah, yeah, yeah, he answered disgustedly.

He forced himself to spend a good amount of time familiarizing himself with the instrument.

He fiddled with the mirror until he could direct a beam of light on the object in a matter of seconds. He acquainted himself with the lenses, varying from a three-inch power to a one-twelfth-inch power. In the case of the latter, he learned to place a drop of cedar-wood oil on the slide, then rack down until the lens touched the oil. He broke thirteen slides doing it.

Within three days of steady attention, he could manipulate the milled adjustment heads rapidly, could control the iris diaphragm and condenser to get exactly the right amount of light on the slide, and was soon getting a sharply defined clarity with the ready-made slides he'd got.

He never knew a flea looked so godawful.

Next came mounting, a process much more difficult, he soon discovered.

No matter how he tried, he couldn't seem to keep dust particles out of the mount. When he looked at them in the microscope, it looked as if he were examining boulders.

It was especially difficult because of the dust storms, which still occurred on an average of once every four days. He was ultimately obliged to build a shelter over the bench.

He also learned to be systematic while experimenting with the mounts. He found that continually searching for things allowed that much more time for dust to accumulate on his slides. Grudgingly, almost amused, he soon had a place for everything. Glass slips, cover glasses, pipettes, cells, forceps, Petri dishes, needles, chemicals – all were placed in systematic locations.

He found, to his surprise, that he actually gleaned pleasure from practicing orderliness. I guess I got old Fritz's blood in me, after all, he thought once in amusement.

Then he got a specimen of blood from a woman.

It took him days to get a few drops properly mounted in a cell, the cell properly centered on the slide. For a while he thought he'd never get it right.

But then the morning came when, casually, as if it were only of minor import, he put his thirty-seventh slide of blood under the lens, turned on the spotlight, adjusted the draw tube and mirror, racked down and adjusted the diaphragm and condenser. Every second that passed seemed to increase the heaviness of his heartbeat, for somehow he knew this was the time.

The moment arrived; his breath caught.

It wasn't a virus, then. You couldn't see a virus. And there, fluttering delicately on the slide, was a germ.

I dub thee *vampiris*. The words crept across his mind as he stood looking down into the eyepiece.

By checking in one of the bacteriology texts, he'd found that the cylindrical bacterium he saw was a bacillus, a tiny rod of protoplasm that moved itself through the blood by means of tiny threads that projected from the cell envelope. These hair-like flagella lashed vigorously at the fluid medium and pro-pelled the bacillus.

For a long time he stood looking into the microscope, unable to think or continue with the investigation.

All he could think was that here, on the slide, was the cause of the vampire. All the centuries of fearful superstition had been felled in the moment he had seen the germ.

The scientists had been right, then; there *were* bacteria involved. It had taken him, Robert Neville, thirty-six, survivor, to complete the inquest and announce the murderer – the germ *within* the vampire.

Suddenly a massive weight of despair fell over him. To have the answer now when it was too late was a crushing blow. He tried desperately to fight the depression, but it held on. He didn't know where to start, he felt utterly helpless before the problem. How could he ever hope to cure those still living? He didn't know anything about bacteria.

Well, I *will* know! he raged inside. And he forced himself to study.

Certain kinds of bacilli, when conditions became unfavorable for life, were capable of creating, from themselves, bodies called spores.

What they did was condense their cell contents into an oval body with a thick wall. This body, when completed, detached itself from the bacillus and became a free spore, highly resistant to physical and chemical change.

Later, when conditions were more favorable for survival, the spore germinated again, bringing into existence all the qualities of the original bacillus.

Robert Neville stood before the sink, eyes closed, hands clasped tightly at the edge. Something there, he told himself forcefully, something there. But *what*?

Suppose, he predicated, the vampire got no blood. Conditions then for the *vampiris* bacillus would be unfavorable.

Protecting itself, the germ sporulates; the vampire sinks into a coma. Finally, when conditions become favorable again, the vampire walks again, its body still the same.

But how would the germ know if blood were available? He slammed a fist on the sink in anger. He read again. There was still something there. He felt it.

Bacteria, when not properly fed, metabolized abnormally and produced bacteriophages (inanimate, self-reproducing proteins). These bacteriophages destroyed the bacteria.

When no blood came in, the bacilli would metabolize abnormally, absorb water, and swell up, ultimately to explode and destroy all cells.

Sporulation again; it had to fit in.

All right, suppose the vampire didn't go into a coma. Suppose its body decomposed without blood. The germ still might sporulate and—

Yes! The dust storms!

The freed spores would be blown about by the storms. They could lodge in minute skin abrasions caused by the scaling dust. Once in the skin, the spore could germinate and multiply by fission. As this multiplication progressed, the surrounding tissues would be destroyed, the channels plugged with bacilli. Destruction of tissue cells and bacilli would liberate poisonous, decomposed bodies into surrounding healthy tissues. Eventually the poisons would reach the blood stream.

Process complete.

And all without blood-eyed vampires hovering over heroines' beds. All without bats fluttering against estate windows, all without the supernatural.

The vampire was real. It was only that his true story had never been told.

Considering that, Neville recounted the historical plagues.

He thought about the fall of Athens. That had been very much like the plague of 1975. Before anything could be done, the city had fallen. Historians wrote of bubonic plague. Robert Neville was inclined to believe that the vampire had caused it.

No, not the vampire. For now, it appeared, that prowling, vulpine ghost was as much a tool of the germ as the living innocents who were originally afflicted. It was the germ that was the villain. The germ that hid behind obscuring veils of legend and superstition, spreading its scourge while people cringed before their own fears.

And what of the Black Plague, that horrible blight that swept across Europe, leaving in its wake a toll of three fourths of the population?

Vampires?

By ten that night, his head ached and his eyes felt like hot blobs of gelatine. He discovered that he was ravenous. He got a steak from the freezer, and while it was broiling he took a fast shower.

He jumped a little when a rock hit the side of the house. Then he grinned wryly. He'd been so absorbed all day that he'd forgotten about the pack of them that prowled around his house.

While he was drying himself, he suddenly realized that he didn't know what portion of the vampires who came nightly were physically alive and what portion were activated entirely by the germ. Odd, he thought, that he didn't know. There had to be both kinds, because some of them he shot without success, while others had been destroyed. He assumed that the dead ones could somehow withstand bullets.

Which brought up another point. Why did the living ones come to his house? Why just those few and not everyone in that area?

He had a glass of wine with his steak and was amazed how flavorsome everything was. Food usually tasted like wood to him. I must have worked up an appetite today, he thought.

Furthermore, he hadn't had a single drink. Even more fantastic, he hadn't wanted one. He shook his head. It was painfully obvious that liquor was an emotional solace to him.

The steak he finished to the bone, and he even chewed on that. Then he took the rest of the wine into the living room, turned on the record player, and sat down in his chair with a tired grunt.

He sat listening to Ravel's Daphnis and Chloe Suites One and Two, all the lights off except the spotlight on the woods. He managed to forget all about vampires for a while.

Later, though, he couldn't resist taking another look in the microscope.

You bastard, he thought, almost affectionately, watching the minuscule protoplasm fluttering on the slide. You dirty little bastard.

CHAPTER TWELVE

The next day stank.

The sun lamp killed the germs on the slide, but that didn't explain anything to him.

He mixed allyl sulphide with the germ-ridden blood and nothing happened. The allyl sulphide was absorbed, the germs still lived.

He paced nervously around the bedroom.

Garlic kept them away and blood was the fulcrum of their existence. Yet, mix the essence of garlic with the blood and nothing happened. His hands closed into angry fists.

Wait a minute; that blood was from one of the living ones.

An hour later he had a sample of the other kind. He mixed it with allyl sulphide and looked at it through the microscope. Nothing happened.

Lunch stuck in his throat.

What about the stake, then? All he could think of was hemorrhage, and he knew it wasn't that. That damned woman . . .

He tried half the afternoon to think of something concrete. Finally, with a snarl, he knocked the microscope over and stalked into the living room. He thudded down onto the chair and sat there, tapping impatient fingers on the arm.

Brilliant, Neville, he thought. You're uncanny. Go to the head of the class. He sat there, biting a knuckle. Let's face it, he thought miserably, I lost my mind a long time ago. I can't think two days in succession without having seams come loose. I'm useless, worthless, without value, a dud.

All right, he replied with a shrug, that settles it. Let's get back to the problem. So he did.

There are certain things established, he lectured himself. There *is* a germ, it's transmitted, sunlight kills it, garlic is effective. Some vampires sleep in soil, the stake destroys them. They don't turn into wolves or bats, but certain animals acquire the germ and become vampires.

All right.

He made a list. One column he headed 'Bacilli,' the other he headed with a question mark.

He began.

The cross. No, that couldn't have anything to do with the bacilli. If anything, it was psychological.

The soil. Could there be something in the soil that affected the germ? No. How would it get in the blood stream? Besides, very few of them slept in the soil.

His throat moved as he added the second item to the column headed by a question mark.

Running water. Could it be absorbed porously and . . . No, that was stupid. They came out in the rain, and they wouldn't if it harmed them. Another notation in the right-hand column. His hand shook a little as he entered it.

Sunlight. He tried vainly to glean satisfaction from putting down one item in the desired column.

The stake. No. His throat moved. Watch it, he warned.

The mirror. For God's sake, how could a mirror have anything to do with germs? His hasty scrawl in the right-hand column was hardly legible. His hand shook a little more.

Garlic. He sat there, teeth gritted. He had to add at least one more item to the bacilli column; it was almost a point of honor. He struggled over the last item. Garlic, garlic. It *must* affect the germ. But how?

He started to write in the right-hand column, but before he could finish, fury came from far down like lava shooting up to the crest of a volcano.

Damn!

81

He crumpled the paper into a ball in his fist and hurled it away. He stood up, rigid and frenzied, looking around. He wanted to break things, anything. So you thought your frenzied period was over, did you! he yelled at himself, lurching forward to fling over the bar.

Then he caught himself and held back. No, no, don't get started, he begged. Two shaking hands ran through his lank blond hair. His throat moved convulsively and he shuddered with the repressed craving for violence.

The sound of the whisky gurgling into the glass angered him. He turned the bottle upside down and the whisky spurted out in great gushes, splashing up the sides of the glass and over onto the mahogany top of the bar.

He swallowed the whole glassful at once, head thrown back, whisky running out the edges of his mouth.

I'm an animal! he exulted. I'm a *dumb, stupid* animal and I'm going to drink!

He emptied the glass, then flung it across the room. It bounced off the bookcase and rolled across the rug. Oh, so you won't break, won't you! he rasped inside his head, leaping across the rug to grind the glass into splinters under his heavy shoes.

Then he spun and stumbled to the bar again. He filled another glass and poured the contents down his throat. I wish I had a pipe with whisky in it! he thought. I'd connect a goddamn hose to it and flush whisky down me until it came out my ears! Until I *floated* in it!

He flung away the glass. Too slow, too *slow*, damn it! He drank directly from the uptilted bottle, gulping furiously, hating himself, punishing himself with the whisky burning down his rapidly swallowing throat.

I'll choke myself! he stormed. I'll strangle myself, I'll *drown* myself in whisky! Like Clarence in his malmsey, I'll die, die, *die*!

He hurled the empty bottle across the room and it shattered on the wall mural. Whisky ran down the tree trunks and onto the ground. He lurched across the room and picked up a piece of the broken bottle. He slashed at the mural and the jagged edge sliced through the scene and peeled it away from the wall. There! he thought, his breath like steam escaping. That for you!

He flung the glass away, then looked down as he felt dull pain in his fingers. He'd sliced open the flesh.

Good! he exulted viciously, and pressed on each side of the slices until the blood ran out and fell in big drops on the rug. Bleed to death, you stupid, worthless bastard!

An hour later he was totally drunk, lying flat on the floor with a vacuous smile on his face.

World's gone to hell. No germs, no science. World's fallen to the supernatural, it's a supernatural world. Harper's Bizarre and Saturday Evening Ghost and Ghoul Housekeeping. 'Young Dr Jekyll' and 'Dracula's Other Wife' and 'Death Can Be Beautiful.' 'Don't be half-staked' and Smith Brothers' Coffin Drops.

He stayed drunk for two days and planned on staying drunk till the end of time or the world's whisky supply, whichever came first.

And he might have done it, too, if it hadn't been for a miracle.

It happened on the third morning, when he stumbled out onto the porch to see if the world was still there.

There was a dog roving about on the lawn.

The second it heard him open the front door, it stopped snuffling over the grass, its head jerked up in sudden fright, and it bounded off to the side with a twitch of scrawny limbs.

For a moment Robert Neville was so shocked he couldn't move. He stood petrified, staring at the dog, which was limping quickly across the street, its ropelike tail pulled between its legs.

It was *alive*! In the *daytime*! He lurched forward with a dull cry and almost pitched on his face on the lawn. His legs pistoned, his arms flailed for balance. Then he caught himself and started running after the dog.

'Hey!' he called, his hoarse voice breaking the silence of Cimarron Street. 'Come back here!'

His shoes thudded across the sidewalk and off the curb,

every step driving a battering ram into his head. His heart pulsed heavily.

'Hey!' he called again. 'Come 'ere, boy.'

Across the street, the dog scrambled unsteadily along the sidewalk, its right hind leg curled up, its dark claws clicking on the cement.

'Come 'ere, boy, I won't hurt you!' Robert Neville called out.

Already he had a stitch in his side and his head throbbed with pain as he ran. The dog stopped a moment and looked back. Then it darted in between two houses, and for a moment Neville saw it from the side. It was brown and white, breedless, its left ear hanging in shreds, its gaunt body wobbling as it ran.

'Don't run away!'

He didn't hear the shrill quiver of hysteria in his voice as he screamed out the words. His throat choked up as the dog disappeared between the houses. With a grunt of fear he hobbled on faster, ignoring the pain of hangover, everything lost in the need to catch that dog.

But when he got into the back yard the dog was gone.

He ran to the redwood fence and looked over. Nothing. He twisted back suddenly to see if the dog were going back out the way it had entered.

There was no dog.

For an hour he wandered around the neighborhood on trembling legs, searching vainly, calling out every few moments, 'Come 'ere, boy, come 'ere.'

At last he stumbled home, his face a mask of hopeless dejection. To come across a living being, after all this time to find a companion, and then to lose it. Even if it was only a dog. *Only* a dog? To Robert Neville that dog was the peak of a planet's evolution.

He couldn't eat or drink anything. He found himself so ill and trembling at the shock and the loss that he had to lie down. But he couldn't sleep. He lay there shaking feverishly, his head moving from side to side on the flat pillow.

'Come 'ere, boy,' he kept muttering without realizing it. 'Come 'ere, boy, I won't hurt you.'

In the afternoon he searched again. For two blocks in each direction from his house he searched each yard, each street, each individual house. But he found nothing.

When he got home, about five, he put out a bowl of milk and a piece of hamburger. He put a ring of garlic bulbs around it, hoping the vampires wouldn't touch it.

But later it came to him that the dog must be afflicted too, and the garlic would keep it away also. He couldn't understand that. If the dog had the germ, how could it roam outdoors during the daylight hours? Unless it had such a small dosing of bacilli in its veins that it wasn't really affected yet. But, if that were true, how had it survived the nightly attacks?

Oh, my God, the thought came then, what if it comes back tonight for the meat and they kill it? What if he went out the next morning and found the dog's body on the lawn and knew that he was responsible for its death? I couldn't take that, he thought miserably. I'll blow out my brains if that happens, I swear I will.

The thought dredged up again the endless enigma of why he went on. All right, there were a few possibilities for experiment now, but life was still a barren, cheerless trial. Despite everything he had or might have (except, of course, another human being), life gave no promise of improvement or even of change. The way things shaped up, he would live out his life with no more than he already had. And how many years was that? Thirty, maybe forty if he didn't drink himself to death.

The thought of forty more years of living as he was made him shudder.

And yet he hadn't killed himself. True, he hardly treated his body welfare with reverence. He didn't eat properly, drink properly, sleep properly, or do anything properly. His health wasn't going to last indefinitely; he was already cheating the percentages, he suspected.

But using his body carelessly wasn't suicide. He'd never even approached suicide. Why?

There seemed no answer. He wasn't resigned to anything, he hadn't accepted or adjusted to the life he'd been forced into. Yet here he was, eight months after the plague's last victim, nine since he'd spoken to another human being, ten since Virginia had died. Here he was with no future and a virtually hopeless present. Still plodding on.

Instinct? Or was he just stupid? Too unimaginative to destroy himself? Why hadn't he done it in the beginning, when he was in the very depths? What had impelled him to enclose the house, install a freezer, a generator, an electric stove, a water tank, build a hothouse, a workbench, burn down the houses on each side of his, collect records and books and mountains of canned supplies, even – it was fantastic when you thought about it – even put a fancy mural on the wall?

Was the life force something more than words, a tangible, mind-controlling potency? Was nature somehow, in him, maintaining its spark against its own encroachments?

He closed his eyes. Why think, why reason? There was no answer. His continuance was an accident and an attendant bovinity. He was just too dumb to end it all, and that was about the size of it.

Later he glued up the sliced mural and put it back into place. The slits didn't show too badly unless he stood very close to the paper.

He tried briefly to get back to the problem of the bacilli, but he realized that he couldn't concentrate on anything except the dog. To his complete astonishment, he later found himself offering up a stumbling prayer that the dog would be protected. It was a moment in which he felt a desperate need to believe in a God that shepherded his own creations. But, even praying, he felt a twinge of self-reproach, and knew he might start mocking his own prayer at any second.

Somehow, though, he managed to ignore his iconoclastic self and went on praying anyway. Because he wanted the dog, because he needed the dog.

CHAPTER THIRTEEN

In the morning when he went outside he found that the milk and hamburger were gone.

His eyes rushed over the lawn. There were two women crumpled on the grass but the dog wasn't there. A breath of relief passed his lips. Thank God for that, he thought. Then he grinned to himself. If I were religious now, he thought, I'd find in this a vindication of my prayer.

Immediately afterward he began berating himself for not being awake when the dog had come. It must have been after dawn, when the streets were safe. The dog must have evolved a system to have lived so long. But he should have been awake to watch.

He consoled himself with the hope that he was winning the dog over, if only with food. He was briefly worried by the idea that the vampires had taken the food, and not the dog. But a quick check ended that fear. The hamburger had not been lifted over the garlic ring, but dragged through it along the cement of the porch. And all around the bowl were tiny milk splashes, still moist, that could have been made only by a dog's lapping tongue.

Before he had breakfast he put out more milk and more hamburger, placing them in the shade so the milk wouldn't get too warm. After a moment's deliberation he also put out a bowl of cold water.

Then, after eating, he took the two women to the fire and, returning, stopped at a market and picked up two dozen cans of the best dog food as well as boxes of dog biscuit, dog candy, dog soap, flea powder, and a wire brush.

Lord, you'd think I was having a baby or something, he thought as he struggled back to the car with his arms full. A grin faltered on his lips. Why pretend? he thought. I'm more excited than I've been in a year. The eagerness he'd felt upon seeing the germ in his microscope was nothing compared with what he felt about the dog.

He drove home at eighty miles an hour, and he couldn't help a groan of disappointment when he saw that the meat and drink were untouched. Well, what the hell do you expect? he asked himself sarcastically. The dog can't eat every hour on the hour.

Putting down the dog food and equipment on the kitchen table, he looked at his watch. Ten-fifteen. The dog would be back when it got hungry again. Patience, he told himself. Get yourself at least *one* virtue, anyway.

He put away the cans and boxes. Then he checked the outside of the house and the hothouse. There was a loose board to fasten and a pane to repair on the hothouse roof.

While he collected garlic bulbs, he wondered once again why the vampires had never set fire to his house. It seemed such an obvious tactic. Was it possible they were afraid of matches? Or was it that they were just too stupid? After all, their brains could not be so fully operative as they had been before. The change from life to mobile death must have involved some tissue deterioration.

No, that theory wasn't any good, because there were living ones around his house at night too. Nothing was wrong with their brains, was there?

He skipped it. He was in no mood for problems. He spent the rest of the morning preparing and hanging garlic strands. Once he wondered about the fact that garlic bulbs worked. In legend it was always the blossoms of the garlic plant. He shrugged. What was the difference? The proof of the garlic was in its chasing ability. He imagined that the blossoms would work too.

After lunch he sat at the peephole looking out at the bowls and the plate. There was no sound anywhere except for the almost inaudible humming of the air-conditioning units in the bedroom, bathroom, and kitchen.

The dog came at four. Neville had almost fallen into a doze as he sat there before the peephole. Then his eyes blinked and focused as the dog came hobbling slowly across the street, looking at the house with white-rimmed, cautious eyes. He wondered what was wrong with the dog's paw. He wanted very much to fix it and get the dog's affection. Shades of Androcles, he thought in the gloom of his house.

He forced himself to sit still and watch. It was incredible, the feeling of warmth and normality it gave him to see the dog slurping up the milk and eating the hamburger, its jaws snapping and popping with relish. He sat there with a gentle smile on his face, a smile he wasn't conscious of. It was such a nice dog.

His throat swallowed convulsively as the dog finished eating and started away from the porch. Jumping up from the stool, he moved quickly for the front door.

Then he held himself back. No, that wasn't the way, he decided reluctantly. You'll just scare him if you go out. Let him go now, let him go.

He went back to the peephole and watched the dog wobbling across the street and moving in between those two houses again. He felt a tightness in his throat as he watched it leave. It's all right, he soothed himself, he'll be back.

He turned away from the peephole and made himself a mild drink. Sitting in the chair and sipping slowly, he wondered where the dog went at night. At first he'd been worried about not having it in the house with him. But then he'd realized that the dog must be a master at hiding itself to have lasted so long.

It was probably, he thought, one of those freak accidents that followed no percentage law. Somehow, by luck, by coincidence, maybe by a little skill, that one dog had survived the plague and the grisly victims of the plague.

That started him thinking. If a dog, with its limited intelligence, could manage to subsist through it all, wouldn't a person with a reasoning brain have that much more chance for survival?

He made himself think about something else. It was dangerous to hope. That was a truism he had long accepted.

The next morning the dog came again. This time Robert Neville opened the front door and went out. The dog immediately bolted away from the dish and bowls, right ear flattened back, legs scrambling frantically across the street.

Neville twitched with the repressed instinct to pursue. As casually as he could manage, he sat down on the edge of the porch.

Across the street the dog ran between the houses again and disappeared. After fifteen minutes of sitting, Neville went in again.

After a small breakfast he put out more food.

The dog came at four and Neville went out again, this time making sure that the dog was finished eating.

Once more the dog fled. But this time, seeing that it was not pursued, it stopped across the street and looked back for a moment.

'It's all right, boy,' Neville called out, but at the sound of his voice the dog ran away again.

Neville sat on the porch stiffly, teeth gritted with impatience. Goddamn it, what's the matter with him? he thought. The damn *mutt*!

He forced himself to think of what the dog must have gone through. The endless nights of groveling in the blackness, hidden God knew where, its gaunt chest laboring in the night while all around its shivering form the vampires walked. The foraging for food and water, the struggle for life in a world without masters, housed in a body that man had made dependent on himself.

Poor little fella, he thought, I'll be good to you when you come and live with me.

Maybe, the thought came then, a dog had *more* chance of survival than a human. Dogs were smaller, they could hide in places the vampires couldn't go. They could probably sense the alien nature of those about them, probably *smell* it.

That didn't make him any happier. For always, in spite of reason, he had clung to the hope that someday he would find someone like himself – a man, a woman, a child, it didn't matter. Sex was fast losing its meaning without the endless prodding of mass hypnosis. Loneliness he still felt.

Sometimes he had indulged in daydreams about finding someone. More often, though, he had tried to adjust to what he sincerely believed was the inevitable – that he was actually the only one left in the world. At least in as much of the world as he could ever hope to know.

Thinking about it, he almost forgot that nightfall was approaching.

With a start he looked up and saw Ben Cortman running at him from across the street.

'Neville!'

He jumped up from the porch and ran into the house, locking and bolting the door behind him with shaking hands.

For a certain period he went out on the porch just as the dog had finished eating. Every time he went out the dog ran away, but as the days passed it ran with decreasing speed, and soon it was stopping halfway across the street to look back and bark at him. Neville never followed, but sat down on the porch and watched. It was a game they played.

Then one day Neville sat on the porch *before* the dog came. And, when it appeared across the street, he remained seated.

For about fifteen minutes the dog hovered near the curb suspiciously, unwilling to approach the food. Neville edged as far away from the food as he could in order to encourage the dog. Unthinking, he crossed his legs, and the dog shrank away at the unexpected motion. Neville held himself quietly then and the dog kept moving around restlessly in the street, its eyes moving from Neville to the food and back again.

'Come on, boy,' Neville said to it. 'Eat your food, that's a good dog.'

Another ten minutes passed. The dog was now on the lawn, moving in concentric arcs that became shorter and shorter.

The dog stopped. Then slowly, very slowly, one paw at a time, it began moving up on the dish and bowls, its eyes never leaving Neville for a second.

'That's the boy,' Neville said quietly.

This time the dog didn't flinch or back away at the sound of his voice. Still Neville made sure he sat motionless so that no abrupt movement would startle the dog.

The dog moved yet closer, stalking the plate, its body tense and waiting for the least motion from Neville.

'That's right,' Neville told the dog.

Suddenly the dog darted in and grabbed the meat. Neville's pleased laughter followed its frantically erratic wobble across the street.

'You little son of a gun,' he said appreciatively.

Then he sat and watched the dog as it ate. It crouched down on a yellow lawn across the street, its eyes on Neville while it wolfed down the hamburger. Enjoy it, he thought, watching the dog. From now on you get dog food. I can't afford to let you have any more fresh meat.

When the dog had finished it straightened up and came across the street again, a little less hesitantly. Neville still sat there, feeling his heart thud nervously. The dog was beginning to trust him and somehow it made him tremble. He sat there, his eyes fastened on the dog.

'That's right, boy,' he heard himself saying aloud. 'Get your water now, that's a good dog.'

A sudden smile of delight raised his lips as he saw the dog's good ear stand up. He's *listening*! he thought excitedly. He hears what I say, the little son of a gun!

'Come on, boy.' He went on talking eagerly. 'Get your water and your milk now, that's a good boy. I won't hurt you. Atta boy.'

The dog went to the water and drank gingerly, its head lifting with sudden jerks to watch him, then dipping down again.

'I'm not doing anything,' Neville told the dog.

He couldn't get over how odd his voice sounded. When a man didn't hear the sound of his own voice for almost a year, it sounded very strange to him. A year was a long time to live in silence. When you come live with me, he thought, I'll talk your ear off.

The dog finished the water.

'Come 'ere, boy,' Neville said invitingly, patting his leg. '*Come* on.'

The dog looked at him curiously, its good ear twitching again. Those eyes, Neville thought. What a world of feeling in those eyes! Distrust, fear, hope, loneliness – all etched in those big brown eyes. Poor little guy.

'Come on, boy, I won't hurt you,' he said gently.

Then he stood up and the dog ran away. Neville stood there looking at the fleeing dog shaking his head slowly.

More days passed. Each day Neville sat on the porch while the dog ate, and before long the dog approached the dish and bowls without hesitation, almost boldly, with the assurance of the dog that knows its human conquest.

And all the time Neville would talk to it.

'That's a good boy. Eat up the food. That's *good* food, isn't it? Sure it is. I'm your friend. I gave you that food. Eat it up, boy, that's right. That's a *good* dog,' endlessly cajoling, praising, pouring soft words into the dog's frightened mind as it ate.

And every day he sat a little bit closer to it, until the day came when he could have reached out and touched the dog if he'd stretched a little. He didn't, though. I'm not taking any chances, he told himself. I don't want to scare him.

But it was hard to keep his hands still. He could almost feel

93

them twitching empathically with his strong desire to reach out and stroke the dog's head. He had such a terrible yearning to love something again, and the dog was such a beautifully ugly dog.

He kept talking to the dog until it became quite used to the sound of his voice. It hardly looked up now when he spoke. It came and went without trepidation, eating and barking its curt acknowledgment from across the street. Soon now, Neville told himself, I'll be able to pat his head. The days passed into pleasant weeks, each hour bringing him closer to a companion.

Then one day the dog didn't come.

Neville was frantic. He'd got so used to the dog's coming and going that it had become the fulcrum of his daily schedule, everything fitting around the dog's mealtimes, investigation forgotten, everything pushed aside but his desire to have the dog in his house.

He spent a nerve-racked afternoon searching the neighborhood, calling out in a loud voice for the dog. But no amount of searching helped, and he went home to a tasteless dinner. The dog didn't come for dinner that night or for breakfast the next morning. Again Neville searched, but with less hope. They've got him, he kept hearing the words in his mind, the dirty bastards have got him. But he couldn't really believe it. He wouldn't let himself believe it.

On the afternoon of the third day he was in the garage when he heard the sound of the metal bowl clinking outside. With a gasp he ran out into the daylight.

'You're *back*!' he cried.

The dog jerked away from the plate nervously, water dripping from its jaws.

Neville's heart leaped. The dog's eyes were glazed and it was panting for breath, its dark tongue hanging out.

'No,' he said, his voice breaking. 'Oh, *no*.'

The dog still backed across the lawn on trembling stalks of legs. Quickly Neville sat down on the porch steps and stayed there trembling. Oh, no, he thought in anguish, oh, God, *no*.

94

He sat there watching it tremble fitfully as it lapped up the water. No. No. It's not true.

'Not true,' he murmured without realizing it.

Then, instinctively, he reached out his hand. The dog drew back a little, teeth bared in a throaty snarl.

'It's all right, boy,' Neville said quietly. 'I won't hurt you.' He didn't even know what he was saying.

He couldn't stop the dog from leaving. He tried to follow it, but it was gone before he could discover where it hid. He'd decided it must be under a house somewhere, but that didn't do him any good.

He couldn't sleep that night. He paced restlessly, drinking pots of coffee and cursing the sluggishness of time. He had to get hold of the dog, he had to. And soon. He had to cure it.

But how? His throat moved. There had to be a way. Even with the little he knew there *must* be a way.

The next morning he sat right beside the bowl and he felt his lips shaking as the dog came limping slowly across the street. It didn't eat anything. Its eyes were more dull and listless than they'd been the day before. Neville wanted to jump at it and try to grab hold of it, take it in the house, nurse it.

But he knew that if he jumped and missed he might undo everything. The dog might never return.

All through the meal his hand kept twitching out to pat the dog's head. But every time it did, the dog cringed away with a snarl. He tried being forceful. '*Stop* that!' he said in a firm, angry tone, but that only frightened the dog more and it drew away farther from him. Neville had to talk to it for fifteen minutes, his voice a hoarse, trembling sound, before the dog would return to the water.

This time he managed to follow the slow-moving dog and saw which house it squirmed under. There was a little metal screen he could have put up over the opening, but he didn't. He didn't want to frighten the dog. And besides, there would be no way of getting the dog then except through the floor, and that would take too long. He had to get the dog fast.

When the dog didn't return that afternoon, he took a dish of milk and put it under the house where the dog was. The next morning the bowl was empty. He was going to put more milk in it when he realized that the dog might never leave his lair then. He put the bowl back in front of his house and prayed that the dog was strong enough to reach it. He was too worried even to criticize his inept prayer.

When the dog didn't come that afternoon he went back and looked in. He paced back and forth outside the opening and almost put milk there anyway. No, the dog would *never* leave then.

He went home and spent a sleepless night. The dog didn't come in the morning. Again he went to the house. He listened at the opening but couldn't hear any sound of breathing. Either it was too far back for him to hear or . . .

He went back to the house and sat on the porch. He didn't have breakfast or lunch. He just sat there.

That afternoon, late, the dog came limping out between the houses, moving slowly on its bony legs. Neville forced himself to sit there without moving until the dog had reached the food. Then, quickly, he reached down and picked up the dog.

Immediately it tried to snap at him, but he caught its jaws in his right hand and held them together. Its lean, almost hairless body squirmed feebly in his grasp and pitifully terrified whines pulsed in its throat.

'It's all right,' he kept saying. 'It's all right, boy.'

Quickly he took it into his room and put it down on the little bed of blankets he'd arranged for the dog. As soon as he took his hand off its jaws the dog snapped at him and he jerked his hand back. The dog lunged over the linoleum with a violent scrabbling of paws, heading for the door. Neville jumped up and blocked its way. The dog's legs slipped on the smooth surface, then it got a little traction and disappeared under the bed.

Neville got on his knees and looked under the bed. In the

gloom there he saw the two glowing coals of eyes and heard the fitful panting.

'*Come* on, boy,' he pleaded unhappily. 'I won't hurt you. You're *sick*. You need help.'

The dog wouldn't budge. With a groan Neville got up finally and went out, closing the door behind him. He went and got the bowls and filled them with milk and water. He put them in the bedroom near the dog's bed.

He stood by his own bed a moment, listening to the panting dog, his face lined with pain.

'Oh,' he muttered plaintively, 'why don't you *trust* me?'

He was eating dinner when he heard the horrible crying and whining.

Heart pounding, he jumped up from the table and raced across the living room. He threw open the bedroom door and flicked on the light.

Over in the corner by the bench the dog was trying to dig a hole in the floor.

Terrified whines shook its body as its front paws clawed frenziedly at the linoleum, slipping futilely on the smoothness of it.

'Boy, it's all right!' Neville said quickly.

The dog jerked around and backed into the corner, hackles rising, jaws drawn back all the way from its yellowish-white teeth, a half-mad sound quivering in its throat.

Suddenly Neville knew what was wrong. It was nighttime and the terrified dog was trying to dig itself a hole to bury itself in.

He stood there helplessly, his brain refusing to work properly as the dog edged away from the corner, then scuttled underneath the workbench.

An idea finally came. Neville moved to his bed quickly and pulled off the top blanket. Returning to the bench, he crouched down and looked under it.

97

The dog was almost flattened against the wall, its body shaking violently, guttural snarls bubbling in its throat.

'All right, boy,' he said. 'All right.'

The dog shrank back as Neville stuck the blanket underneath the bench and then stood up. Neville went over to the door and remained there a minute looking back. If only I could *do* something, he thought helplessly. But I can't even get close to him.

Well, he decided grimly, if the dog didn't accept him soon, he'd have to try a little chloroform. Then he could at least work on the dog, fix its paw and try somehow to cure it.

He went back to the kitchen but he couldn't eat. Finally he dumped the contents of his plate into the garbage disposal and poured the coffee back into the pot. In the living room he made himself a drink and downed it. It tasted flat and unappetizing. He put down the glass and went back to the bedroom with a somber face.

The dog had dug itself under the folds of the blanket and there it was still shaking, whining ceaselessly. No use trying to work on it now, he thought; it's too frightened.

He walked back to the bed and sat down. He ran his hands through his hair and then put them over his face. Cure it, cure it, he thought, and one of his hands bunched into a fist to strike feebly at the mattress.

Reaching out abruptly, he turned off the light and lay down fully clothed. Still lying down, he worked off his sandals and listened to them thump on the floor.

Silence. He lay there staring at the ceiling. Why don't I get up? he wondered. Why don't I try to *do* something?

He turned on his side. Get some sleep. The words came automatically. He knew he wasn't going to sleep, though. He lay in the darkness listening to the dog's whimpering. Die, it's going to die, he kept thinking, there's nothing in the world I can do.

At last, unable to bear the sound, he reached over and switched on the bedside lamp. As he moved across the room

in his stocking feet, he heard the dog trying suddenly to jerk
loose from the blanketing. But it got all tangled up in the folds
and began yelping, terror-stricken, while its body flailed wildly
under the wool.

Neville knelt beside it and put his hands on its body. He
heard the choking snarl and the muffled click of its teeth as it
snapped at him through the blanket.

'All right,' he said. 'Stop it now.'

The dog kept struggling against him, its high-pitched whining never stopping, its gaunt body shaking without control.
Neville kept his hands firmly on its body, pinning it down,
talking to it quietly, gently.

'It's all right now, fella, *all* right. Nobody's going to hurt
you. Take it easy, now. Come on, relax, now. Come on, boy.
Take it easy. Relax. That's right, relax. That's it. Calm down.
Nobody's going to hurt you. We'll take care of you.'

He went on talking intermittently for almost an hour, his
voice a low, hypnotic murmuring in the silence of the room.
And slowly, hesitantly, the dog's trembling eased off. A smile
faltered on Neville's lips as he went on talking, talking.

'That's right. Take it easy, now. We'll take care of you.'

Soon the dog lay still beneath his strong hands, the only
movement its harsh breathing. Neville began patting its head,
began running his right hand over its body, stroking and
soothing.

'That's a good dog,' he said softly. '*Good* dog. I'll take care of
you now. Nobody will hurt you. You understand, don't you,
fella? Sure you do. Sure. You're *my* dog, aren't you?'

Carefully he sat down on the cool linoleum, still patting the
dog.

'You're a good dog, a *good* dog.'

His voice was calm, it was quiet with resignation.

After about an hour he picked up the dog. For a moment it
struggled and started whining, but Neville talked to it again
and it soon calmed down.

He sat down on his bed and held the blanket-covered dog

in his lap. He sat there for hours holding the dog, patting and stroking and talking. The dog lay immobile in his lap, breathing easier.

It was about eleven that night when Neville slowly undid the blanket folds and exposed the dog's head.

For a few minutes it cringed away from his hand, snapping a little. But he kept talking to it quietly, and after a while his hand rested on the warm neck and he was moving his fingers gently, scratching and caressing.

He smiled down at the dog, his throat moving.

'You'll be all better soon,' he whispered. 'Real soon.'

The dog looked up at him with its dulled, sick eyes and then its tongue faltered out and licked roughly and moistly across the palm of Neville's hand.

Something broke in Neville's throat. He sat there silently while tears ran slowly down his cheeks.

In a week the dog was dead.

CHAPTER FOURTEEN

There was no debauch of drinking. Far from it. He found that he actually drank less. Something had changed. Trying to analyze it, he came to the conclusion that his last drunk had put him on the bottom, at the very nadir of frustrated despair. Now, unless he put himself under the ground, the only way he could go was up.

After the first few weeks of building up intense hope about the dog, it had slowly dawned on him that intense hope was not the answer and never had been. In a world of monotonous horror there could be no salvation in wild dreaming. Horror he had adjusted to. But monotony was the greater obstacle, and he realized it now, understood it at long last. And understanding it seemed to give him a sort of quiet peace, a sense of having spread all the cards on his mental table, examined them, and settled conclusively on the desired hand.

Burying the dog had not been the agony he had supposed it would be. In a way, it was almost like burying threadbare hopes and false excitements. From that day on he learned to accept the dungeon he existed in, neither seeking to escape with sudden derring-do nor beating his pate bloody on its walls.

And, thus resigned, he returned to work.

It had happened almost a year before, several days after he had put Virginia to her second and final rest.

Hollow and bleak, a sense of absolute loss in him, he was

walking the streets late one afternoon, hands listless at his sides, feet shuffling with the rhythm of despair. His face mirrored nothing of the helpless agony he felt. His face was a blank.

He had wandered through the streets for hours, neither knowing nor caring where he was going. All he knew was that he couldn't return to the empty rooms of the house, couldn't look at the things they had touched and held and known with him. He couldn't look at Kathy's empty bed, at her clothes hanging still and useless in the closet, couldn't look at the bed that he and Virginia had slept in, at Virginia's clothes, her jewelry, all her perfumes on the bureau. He couldn't go near the house.

And so he walked and wandered, and he didn't know where he was when the people started milling past him, when the man caught his arm and breathed garlic in his face.

'Come, brother, come,' the man said, his voice a grating rasp. He saw the man's throat moving like clammy turkey skin, the red-splotched cheeks, the feverish eyes, the black suit, unpressed, unclean. 'Come and be saved, brother, *saved*.'

Robert Neville stared at the man. He didn't understand. The man pulled him on, his fingers like skeleton fingers on Neville's arm,

'It's never too late, brother,' said the man. 'Salvation comes to him who . . .'

The last of his words were lost now in the rising murmur of sound from the great tent they were approaching. It sounded like the sea imprisoned under canvas, roaring to escape. Robert Neville tried to loose his arm.

'I don't want to—'

The man didn't hear. He pulled Neville on with him and they walked toward the waterfall of crying and stamping. The man did not let go. Robert Neville felt as if he were being dragged into a tidal wave.

'But I don't—'

The tent had swallowed him then, the ocean of shouting, stamping, hand-clapping sound engulfed him. He flinched instinctively and felt his heart begin pumping heavily. He was surrounded now by people, hundreds of them, swelling and gushing around him like waters closing in. And yelling and clapping and crying out words Robert Neville couldn't understand.

Then the cries died down and he heard the voice that stabbed through the half-light like knifing doom, that crackled and bit shrilly over the loud-speaker system.

'Do you want to fear the holy cross of God? Do you want to look into the mirror and not see the face that almighty God has given you? Do you want to come crawling back from the grave like a monster out of hell?'

The voice enjoined hoarsely, pulsing, driving.

'Do you want to be changed into a black unholy animal? Do you want to stain the evening sky with hell-born bat wings? I ask you – do you want to be turned into godless, night-cursed husks, into creatures of eternal damnation?'

'No!' the people erupted, terror-stricken. 'No, *save* us!'

Robert Neville backed away, bumping into flailing-handed, white-jawed true believers screaming out for succor from the lowering skies.

'Well, I'm *telling* you! I'm *telling* you, so listen to the word of God! Behold, evil shall go forth from nation to nation and the slain of the Lord shall be at that day from one end of the earth even unto the other end of the earth! Is that a lie, is that a *lie*?'

'No! *No!*'

'I tell you that unless we become as little children, stainless and pure in the eyes of Our Lord – unless we stand up and shout out the glory of Almighty God and of His only begotten son, Jesus Christ, our Saviour – unless we fall on our *knees* and beg forgiveness for our grievous offenses – we are damned! I'll say it again, so *listen!* We are damned, we are damned, *we are damned*!

'Amen!'

'*Save us!*'

The people twisted and moaned and smote their brows and shrieked in mortal terror and screamed out terrible hallelujahs.

Robert Neville was shoved about, stumbling and lost in a treadmill of hopes, in a crossfire of frenzied worship.

'God has punished us for our great transgressions! God has unleashed the terrible force of His almighty wrath! God has set loose the second deluge upon us – a deluge, a flood, a world-consuming torrent of creatures from *hell*! He has opened the grave, He has unsealed the crypt, He has turned the dead from their black tombs – *and set them upon us*! And death and hell delivered up the dead which were in them! That's the word of God! O God, You have punished us, O God, You have seen the terrible face of our transgressions, O God, You have struck us with the might of Your almighty wrath!'

Clapping hands like the spatter of irregular rifle fire, swaying bodies like stalks in a terrible wind, moans of the great potential dead, screams of the fighting living. Robert Neville strained through their violent ranks, face white, hands before him like those of a blind man seeking shelter.

He escaped, weak and trembling, stumbling away from them. Inside the tent the people screamed. But night had already fallen.

He thought about that now as he sat in the living room nursing a mild drink, a psychology text resting on his lap.

A quotation had started the train of thought, sending him back to that evening ten months before, when he'd been pulled into the wild revival meeting.

'This condition, known as hysterical blindness, may be partial or complete, including one, several, or all objects.'

That was the quotation he'd read. It had started him working on the problem again.

A new approach now. Before, he had stubbornly persisted in attributing all vampire phenomena to the germ. If certain of these phenomena did not fit in with the bacilli, he felt inclined to judge their cause as superstition. True, he'd vaguely considered psychological explanations, but he'd never really given much credence to such a possibility. Now, released at last from unyielding preconceptions, he did.

There was no reason, he knew, why some of the phenomena could not be physically caused, the rest psychological. And, now that he accepted it, it seemed one of those patent answers that only a blind man would miss. Well, I always was the blind-man type, he thought in quiet amusement.

Consider, he thought then, the shock undergone by a victim of the plague.

Toward the end of the plague, yellow journalism had spread a cancerous dread of vampires to all corners of the nation. He could remember himself the rash of pseudo-scientific articles that veiled an out-and-out fright campaign designed to sell papers.

There was something grotesquely amusing in that; the frenetic attempt to sell papers while the world died. Not that all newspapers had done that. Those papers that had lived in honesty and integrity died the same way.

Yellow journalism, though, *had* been rampant in the final days. And, in addition, a great upsurge in revivalism had occurred. In a typical desperation for quick answers, easily understood, people had turned to primitive worship as the solution. With less than success. Not only had they died as quickly as the rest of the people, but they had died with terror in their hearts, with a mortal dread flowing in their very veins.

And then, Robert Neville thought, to have this hideous dread vindicated. To regain consciousness beneath hot, heavy soil and know that death had not brought rest. To find them-selves clawing up through the earth, their bodies driven now by a strange, hideous need.

Such traumatic shocks could undo what mind was left. And such shocks could explain much.

The cross, first of all.

Once they were forced to accept vindication of the dread of being repelled by an object that had been a focal point of worship, their minds could have snapped. Dread of the cross sprang up. And, driven on despite already created dreads, the vampire could have acquired an intense mental loathing, and this self-hatred could have set up a block in their weakened minds causing them to be blind to their own abhorred image. It could make them lonely, soul-lost slaves of the night, afraid to approach anyone, living a solitary existence, often seeking solace in the soil of their native land, struggling to gain a sense of communion with something, with anything.

The water? That he *did* accept as superstition, a carryover of the traditional legend that witches were incapable of crossing running water, as written down in the story of Tam O'Shanter. Witches, vampires – in all these feared beings there was a sort of interwoven kinship. Legends and superstitions could overlap, and did.

And the living vampires? That was simple too now.

In life there were the deranged, the insane. What better hold than vampirism for these to catch on to? He was certain that all the living who came to his house at night were insane, thinking themselves true vampires although actually they were only demented sufferers. And that would explain the fact that they'd never taken the obvious step of burning his house. They simply could not think that logically.

He remembered the man who one night had climbed to the top of the light post in front of the house and, while Robert Neville had watched through the peephole, had leaped into space, waving his arms frantically. Neville hadn't been able to explain it at the time, but now the answer seemed obvious. The man had thought he was a bat.

Neville sat looking at the half-finished drink, a thin smile fastened to his lips.

So, he thought, slowly, surely, we find out about them. Find out that they are no invincible race. Far from it; they are a highly perishable race requiring the strictest of physical conditions for the furtherance of their Godforsaken existence.

He put the drink down on the table.

I don't need it, he thought. My emotions don't need feeding any more. I don't need liquor for forgetting or for escaping. I don't have to escape from anything. Not now.

For the first time since the dog had died he smiled and felt within himself a quiet, well-modulated satisfaction. There were still many things to learn, but not so many as before. Strangely, life was becoming almost bearable. I don the robe of hermit without a cry, he thought.

On the phonograph, music played, quiet and unhurried.

Outside, the vampires waited.

PART 3: JUNE 1978

CHAPTER FIFTEEN

He was out hunting for Cortman. It had become a relaxing hobby, hunting for Cortman; one of the few diversions left to him. On those days when he didn't care to leave the neighborhood and there was no demanding work to be done on the house, he would search. Under cars, behind bushes, under houses, up fireplaces, in closets, under beds, in refrigerators; any place into which a moderately corpulent male body could conceivably be squeezed.

Ben Cortman could be in any one of those places at one time or another. He changed his hiding place constantly. Neville felt certain that Cortman knew he was singled out for capture. He felt, further, that Cortman relished the peril of it. If the phrase were not such an obvious anachronism, Neville would have said that Ben Cortman had a zest for life. Sometimes he thought Cortman was happier now than he ever had been before.

Neville ambled slowly up Compton Boulevard toward the next house he meant to search. An uneventful morning had passed. Cortman was not found, even though Neville knew he was somewhere in the neighborhood. He had to be, because he was always the first one at the house at night. The other ones were almost always strangers. Their turnover was great, because they invariably stayed in the neighborhood and Neville found them and destroyed them. Not Cortman.

As he strolled, Neville wondered again what he'd do if he found Cortman. True, his plan had always been the same:

immediate disposal. But that was on the surface. He knew it wouldn't be that easy. Oh, it wasn't that he felt anything toward Cortman. It wasn't even that Cortman represented a part of the past. The past was dead and he knew it and accepted it.

No, it wasn't either of those things. What it probably was, Neville decided, was that he didn't want to cut off a recreational activity. The rest were such dull, robot-like creatures. Ben, at least, had some imagination. For some reason, his brain hadn't weakened like the others'. It could be, Neville often theorized, that Ben Cortman was born to be dead. Undead, that is, he thought, a wry smile playing on his full lips.

It no longer occurred to him that Cortman was out to kill him. That was a negligible menace.

Neville sank down on the next porch with a slow groan. Then, reaching lethargically into his pocket, he took out his pipe. With an idle thumb he tamped rough tobacco shreds down into the pipe bowl. In a few moments smoke swirls were floating lazily about his head in the warm, still air.

It was a bigger, more relaxed Neville that gazed out across the wide field on the other side of the boulevard. An evenly paced hermit life had increased his weight to 230 pounds. His face was full, his body broad and muscular underneath the loose-fitting denim he wore. He had long before given up shaving. Only rarely did he crop his thick blond beard, so that it remained two to three inches from his skin. His hair was thinning and was long and straggly. Set in the deep tan of his face, his blue eyes were calm and unexcitable.

He leaned back against the brick step, puffing out slow clouds of smoke. Far out across that field he knew there was still a depression in the ground where he had buried Virginia, where she had unburied herself. But knowing it brought no glimmer of reflective sorrow to his eyes. Rather than go on suffering, he had learned to stultify himself to introspection. Time had lost its multidimensional scope. There was only the present for Robert Neville; a present based on day-to-day

survival marked by neither heights of joy nor depths of despair.
I am predominantly vegetable, he often thought to himself.
That was the way he wanted it.

Robert Neville sat gazing at the white spot out in the field for
several minutes before he realized that it was moving.

His eyes blinked once and the skin tightened over his face.
He made a slight sound in his throat, a sound of doubting
question. Then, standing up, he raised his left hand to shade
the sunlight from his eyes.

His teeth bit convulsively into the pipestem.

A woman.

He didn't even try to catch the pipe when it fell from his
mouth as his jaw went slack. For a long, breathless moment, he
stood there on the porch step, staring.

He closed his eyes, opened them. She was still there. Robert
Neville felt the increasing thud in his chest as he watched the
woman.

She didn't see him. Her head was down as she walked across
the long field. He could see her reddish hair blowing in the
breeze, her arms swinging loosely at her sides. His throat
moved. It was such an incredible sight after three years that
his mind could not assimilate it. He kept blinking and staring
as he stood motionless in the shade of the house.

A woman. Alive. *In the daylight.*

He stood, mouth partly open, gaping at the woman. She was
young, he could see now as she came closer; probably in her
twenties. She wore a wrinkled and dirty white dress. She was
very tan, her hair was red. In the dead silence of the afternoon
Neville thought he heard the crunch of her shoes in the long
grass.

I've gone mad. The words presented themselves abruptly.
He felt less shock at that possibility than he did at the notion
that she was real. He had, in fact, been vaguely preparing
himself for just such a delusion. It seemed feasible. The man
who died of thirst saw mirages of lakes. Why shouldn't a man

who thirsted for companionship see a woman walking in the sun?

He started suddenly. No, it wasn't that. For, unless his delusion had sound as well as sight, he now heard her walking through the grass. He knew it was real. The movement of her hair, of her arms. She still looked at the ground. Who was she? Where was she going? Where had she been?

He didn't know what welled up in him. It was too quick to analyze, an instinct that broke through every barrier of time-erected reserve.

His left arm went up.

'Hi!' he cried. He jumped down to the sidewalk. '*Hi*, there!'

A moment of sudden, complete silence. Her head jerked up and they looked at each other. Alive, he thought. Alive!

He wanted to shout more, but he felt suddenly choked up. His tongue felt wooden, his brain refused to function. Alive. The word kept repeating itself in his mind. Alive, alive, alive . . .

With a sudden twisting motion the young woman turned and began running wildly back across the field.

For a moment Neville stood there twitching, uncertain of what to do. Then his heart seemed to burst and he lunged across the sidewalk. His boots jolted down into the street and thudded across.

'Wait!' he heard himself cry.

The woman did not wait. He saw her bronze legs pumping as she fled across the uneven surface of the field. And suddenly he realized that words could not stop her. He thought of how shocked he had been at seeing her. How much more shocked she must have felt hearing a sudden shout end long silence and seeing a great, bearded man waving at her!

His legs drove him up over the other curb and into the field. His heart was pounding heavily now. She's alive! He couldn't stop thinking that. Alive. *A woman alive!*

She couldn't run as fast as he could. Almost immediately

Neville began catching up with her. She glanced back over her shoulder with terrified eyes.

'I won't hurt you!' he cried, but she kept running.

Suddenly she tripped and went crashing down on one knee. Her face turned again and he saw the twisted fright on it.

'I won't *hurt* you!' he yelled again.

With a desperate lunge she regained her footing and ran on.

No sound now but the sound of her shoes and his boots thrashing through the heavy grass. He began jumping over the grass to avoid its impending height and gained more ground. The skirt of her dress whipped against the grass, holding her back.

'Stop!' he cried, again, but more from instinct than with any hope that she would stop.

She didn't. She ran still faster and, gritting his teeth, Neville put another burst of speed into his pursuit. He followed in a straight line as the girl weaved across the field, her light reddish hair billowing behind her.

Now he was so close he could hear her tortured breathing. He didn't like to frighten her, but he couldn't stop now. Everything else in the world seemed to have fallen from view but her. He had to catch her.

His long, powerful legs pistoned on, his boots thudded on the earth.

Another stretch of field. The two of them ran, panting. She glanced back at him again to see how close he was. He didn't realize how frightening he looked; six foot three in his boots, a gigantic bearded man with an intent look.

Now his hand lurched out and he caught her by the right shoulder.

With a gasping scream the young woman twisted away and stumbled to the side. Losing balance, she fell on one hip on the rocky ground. Neville jumped forward to help her up. She scuttled back over the ground and tried to get up, but she slipped and fell again, this time on her back. Her skirt jerked up over her knees. She shoved herself up with a breathless whimper, her dark eyes terrified.

'Here,' he gasped, reaching out his hand.

She slapped it aside with a slight cry and struggled to her feet. He caught her by the arm and her free hand lashed out, raking jagged nails across his forehead and right temple. With a grunt he jerked back his arm and she whirled and began running again.

Neville jumped forward again and caught her by the shoulders.

'What are you afraid—'

He couldn't finish. Her hand drove stingingly across his mouth. Then there was only the sound of gasping and struggling, of their feet scrabbling and slipping on the earth, crackling down the thick grass.

'Will you *stop*!' he cried, but she kept battling.

She jerked back and his taut fingers ripped away part of her dress. He let go and the material fluttered down to her waist. He saw her tanned shoulder and the white brassiere cup over her left breast.

She clawed out at him and he caught her wrists in an iron grip. Her right foot drove a bone-numbing kick to his shin.

'Damn it!'

With a snarl of rage he drove his right palm across her face. She staggered back, then looked at him dizzily. Abruptly she started crying helplessly. She sank to her knees before him, holding her arms over her head as if to ward off further blows.

Neville stood there gasping, looking down at her cringing form. He blinked, then took a deep breath.

'Get up,' he said. 'I'm not going to *hurt* you.'

She didn't raise her head. He looked down confusedly at her. He didn't know what to say.

'I said I'm not going to hurt you,' he told her again.

She looked up. But his face seemed to frighten her again, for she shrank back. She crouched there looking up at him fearfully.

'What are you afraid of?' he asked.

He didn't realize that his voice was devoid of warmth, that it was the harsh, sterile voice of a man who had lost all touch with humanity.

He took a step toward her and she drew back again with a frightened gasp. He extended his hand.

'Here,' he said. 'Stand up.'

She got up slowly but without his help. Noticing suddenly her exposed breast, she reached down and held up the torn material of her dress.

They stood there breathing harshly and looking at each other. And, now that the first shock had passed, Neville didn't know what to say. He'd been dreaming of this moment for years. His dreams had never been like this.

'What . . . what's your name?' he asked.

She didn't answer. Her eyes stayed on his face, her lips kept trembling.

'Well?' he asked loudly, and she flinched.

'R-Ruth.' Her voice faltered.

A shudder ran through Robert Neville's body. The sound of her voice seemed to loosen everything in him. Questions disappeared. He felt his heart beating heavily. He almost felt as if he were going to cry.

His hand moved out, almost unconsciously. Her shoulder trembled under his palm.

'Ruth,' he said in a flat, lifeless voice.

His throat moved as he stared at her.

'Ruth,' he said again.

The two of them, the man and the woman, stood facing each other in the great, hot field.

CHAPTER SIXTEEN

The woman lay motionless on his bed, sleeping. It was past four in the afternoon. At least twenty times Neville had stolen into the bedroom to look at her and see if she were awake. Now he sat in the kitchen drinking coffee and worrying.

What if she *is* infected, though? he argued with himself.

The worry had started a few hours before, while Ruth was sleeping. Now, he couldn't rid himself of the fear. No matter how he reasoned, it didn't help. All right, she was tanned from the sun, she had been walking in the daylight. The dog had been in the daylight too.

Neville's fingers tapped restlessly on the table.

Simplicity had departed; the dream had faded into disturbing complexity. There had been no wondrous embrace, no magic words spoken. Beyond her name he had got nothing from her. Getting her to the house had been a battle. Getting her to enter had been even worse. She had cried and begged him not to kill her. No matter what he said to her, she kept crying and begging. He had visualized something on the order of a Hollywood production; stars in their eyes, entering the house, arms about each other, fade-out. Instead he had been forced to tug and cajole and argue and scold while she held back. The entrance had been less than romantic. He had to drag her in.

Once in the house, she had been no less frightened. He'd tried to act comfortingly, but all she did was cower in one corner the way the dog had done. She wouldn't eat or drink anything he gave her. Finally he'd been compelled to take her in the bedroom and lock her in. Now she was asleep.

He sighed wearily and fingered the handle of his cup.

All these years, he thought, dreaming about a companion. Now I meet one and the first thing I do is distrust her, treat her crudely and impatiently.

And yet there was really nothing else he could do. He had accepted too long the proposition that he was the only normal person left. It didn't matter that she looked normal. He'd seen too many of them lying in their coma that looked as healthy as she. They weren't, though, and he knew it. The simple fact that she had been walking in the sunlight wasn't enough to tip the scales on the side of trusting acceptance. He had doubted too long. His concept of the society had become ironbound. It was almost impossible for him to believe that there were others like him. And, after the first shock had diminished, all the dogma of his long years alone had asserted itself.

With a heavy breath he rose and went back to the bedroom. She was still in the same position. Maybe, he thought, she's gone back into coma again.

He stood over the bed, staring down at her. Ruth. There was so much about her he wanted to know. And yet he was almost afraid to find out. Because if she were like the others, there was only one course open. And it was better not to know anything about the people you killed.

His hands twitched at his sides, his blue eyes gazed flatly at her. What if it had been a freak occurrence? What if she had snapped out of coma for a little while and gone wandering? It seemed possible. And yet, as far as he knew, daylight was the one thing the germ could not endure. Why wasn't that enough to convince him she was normal?

Well, there was only one way to make sure.

He bent over and put his hand on her shoulder.

'Wake up,' he said.

She didn't stir. His mouth tightened and his fingers drew in on her soft shoulder.

Then he noticed the thin golden chain around her throat. Reaching in with rough fingers, he drew it out of the bosom of her dress.

He was looking at the tiny gold cross when she woke up and recoiled into the pillow. She's not in coma; that was all he thought.

'What are you d-doing?' she asked faintly.

It was harder to distrust her when she spoke. The sound of the human voice was so strange to him that it had a power over him it had never had before.

'I'm . . . Nothing,' he said.

Awkwardly he stepped back and leaned against the wall. He looked at her a moment longer. Then he asked,

'Where are you from?'

She lay there looking blankly at him.

'I asked you where you were from,' he said.

Again she said nothing. He pushed himself away from the wall with a tight look on his face.

'Ing-Inglewood,' she said hastily.

He looked at her coldly for a moment, then leaned back against the wall.

'I see,' he said. 'Did . . . did you live alone?'

'I was married.'

'Where is your husband?'

Her throat moved. 'He's dead.'

'For how long?'

'Last week.'

'And what did you do after he died?'

'Ran.' She bit into her lower lip. 'I ran away.'

'You mean you've been wandering all this time?'

'Y-yes.'

He looked at her without a word. Then abruptly he turned and his boots thumped loudly as he walked into the kitchen. Pulling open a cabinet door, he drew down a handful of garlic cloves. He put them on a dish, tore them into pieces, and mashed them to a pulp. The acrid fumes assailed his nostrils.

She was propped up on one elbow when he came back. Without hesitation he pushed the dish almost to her face.

She turned her head away with a faint cry.

'What are you doing?' she asked, and coughed once.

'Why do you turn away?'

'Please . . .'

'Why do you turn away?'

'It *smells*!' Her voice broke into a sob. 'Don't! You're making me sick!'

He pushed the plate still closer to her face. With a gagging sound she backed away and pressed against the wall, her legs drawn up on the bed.

'Stop it! *Please!*' she begged.

He drew back the dish and watched her body twitching as her stomach convulsed.

'You're one of them,' he said to her, quietly venomous.

She sat up suddenly and ran past him into the bathroom. The door slammed behind her and he could hear the sound of her terrible retching.

Thin-lipped, he put the dish down on the bedside table. His throat moved as he swallowed.

Infected. It had been a clear sign. He had learned over a year before that garlic was an allergen to any system infected with the *vampiris* bacillus. When the system was exposed to garlic, the stimulated tissues sensitized the cells, causing an abnormal reaction to any further contact with garlic. That was why putting it into their veins had accomplished little. They had to be exposed to the odor.

He sank down on the bed. And the woman had reacted in the wrong way.

After a moment Robert Neville frowned. If what she had said was true, she'd been wandering around for a week. She would naturally be exhausted and weak, and under those conditions the smell of so much garlic *could* have made her retch.

His fist thudded down onto the mattress. He still didn't

know, then, not for certain. And, objectively, he knew he had no right to decide on inadequate evidence. It was something he'd learned the hard way, something he knew and believed absolutely.

He was still sitting there when she unlocked the bathroom door and came out. She stood in the hall a moment looking at him, then went into the living room. He rose and followed. When he came into the living room she was sitting on the couch.

'Are you satisfied?' she asked.

'Never mind that,' he said. 'You're on trial, not me.'

She looked up angrily as if she meant to say something. Then her body slumped and she shook her head. He felt a twinge of sympathy for a moment. She looked so helpless, her thin hands resting on her lap. She didn't seem to care any more about her torn dress. He looked at the slight swelling of her breast. Her figure was very slim, almost curveless. Not at all like the woman he'd used to envision. Never mind that, he told himself, that doesn't matter any more.

He sat down in the chair and looked across at her. She didn't return his gaze.

'Listen to me,' he said then. 'I have every reason to suspect you of being infected. Especially now that you've reacted in such a way to garlic.'

She said nothing.

'Haven't you anything to say?' he asked.

She raised her eyes.

'You think I'm one of them,' she said.

'I think you *might* be.'

'And what about this?' she asked, holding up her cross.

'That means nothing,' he said.

'I'm awake,' she said. 'I'm not in a coma.'

He said nothing. It was something he couldn't argue with, even though it didn't assuage doubt.

'I've been in Inglewood many times,' he said finally. 'Why didn't you hear my car?'

'Inglewood is a big place,' she said.

He looked at her carefully, his fingers tapping on the arm of the chair.

'I'd . . . like to believe you,' he said.

'Would you?' she asked. Another stomach contraction bit her and she bent over with a gasp, teeth clenched. Robert Neville sat there wondering why he didn't feel more compassion for her. Emotion was a difficult thing to summon from the dead, though. He had spent it all and felt hollow now, without feeling.

After a moment she looked up. Her eyes were hard.

'I've had a weak stomach all my life,' she said. 'I saw my husband killed last week. Torn to pieces. Right in front of my eyes I saw it. I lost two children to the plague. And for the past week I've been wandering all over. Hiding at night, not eating more than a few scraps of food. Sick with fear, unable to sleep more than a couple of hours at a time. Then I hear someone shout at me. You chase me over a field, hit me, drag me to your house. Then when I get sick because you shove a plate of reeking garlic in my face, you tell me I'm infected!'

Her hands twitched in her lap.

'What do you *expect* to happen?' she said angrily.

She slumped back against the couch back and closed her eyes. Her hands picked nervously at her skirt. For a moment she tried to tuck in the torn piece, but it fell down again and she sobbed angrily.

He leaned forward in the chair. He was beginning to feel guilty now, in spite of suspicions and doubts. He couldn't help it. He had forgotten about sobbing women. He raised a hand slowly to his beard and plucked confusedly as he watched her.

'Would . . .' he started. He swallowed. 'Would you let me take a sample of your blood?' he asked. 'I could—'

She stood up suddenly and stumbled toward the door. He got up quickly.

'What are you doing?' he asked.

She didn't answer. Her hands fumbled awkwardly with the lock.

'You can't go out there,' he said, surprised. 'The street will be full of them in a little while.'

'I'm not staying here,' she sobbed. 'What's the difference if they kill me?'

His hands closed over her arm. She tried to pull away.

'Leave me alone!' she cried. 'I didn't ask to come here. You dragged me here. Why don't you leave me alone?'

He stood by her awkwardly, not knowing what to say.

'You can't go out,' he said again.

He led her back to the couch. Then he went and got her a small tumbler of whisky at the bar. Never mind whether she's infected or not, he thought, never mind.

He handed her the tumbler. She shook her head.

'Drink it,' he said. 'It'll calm you down.'

She looked up angrily. 'So you can shove more garlic in my face?'

He shook his head.

'Drink it now,' he said.

After a few moments she took the glass and took a sip of the whisky. It made her cough. She put the tumbler on the arm of the couch and a deep breath shook her body.

'Why do you want me to stay?' she asked unhappily.

He looked at her without a definite answer in his mind. Then he said, 'Even if you *are* infected, I can't let you go out there. You don't know what they'd do to you.'

Her eyes closed. 'I don't care,' she said.

CHAPTER SEVENTEEN

'I don't understand it,' he told her over supper. 'Almost three years now, and still there are some of them alive. Food supplies are being used up. As far as I know, they still lie in a coma during the day.' He shook his head. 'But they're not dead. Three years and they're not dead. What keeps them going?'

She was wearing his bathrobe. About five she had relented, taken a bath, and changed. Her slender body was shapeless in the voluminous terry-cloth folds. She'd borrowed his comb and drawn her hair back into a ponytail fastened with a piece of twine.

Ruth fingered her coffee cup.

'We used to see them sometimes,' she said. 'We were afraid to go near them, though. We didn't think we should touch them.'

'Didn't you know they'd come back after they died?'

She shook her head. 'No.'

'Didn't you wonder about the people who attacked your house at night?'

'It never entered our minds that they were . . .' She shook her head slowly. 'It's hard to believe something like that.'

'I suppose,' he said.

He glanced at her as they sat eating silently. It was hard too to believe that here was a normal woman. Hard to believe that, after all these years, a companion had come. It was more than just doubting her. It was doubting that anything so remarkable could happen in such a lost world.

'Tell me more about them,' Ruth said.

He got up and took the coffeepot off the stove. He poured

more into her cup, into his, then replaced the pot and sat down.

'How do you feel now?' he asked her.

'I feel better, thank you.'

He nodded and spooned sugar into his coffee. He felt her eyes on him as he stirred. What's she thinking? he wondered. He took a deep breath, wondering why the tightness in him didn't break. For a while he'd thought that he trusted her. Now he wasn't sure.

'You still don't trust me,' she said, seeming to read his mind.

He looked up quickly, then shrugged.

'It's . . . not that,' he said.

'Of course it is,' she said quietly. She sighed. 'Oh, very well. If you have to check my blood, check it.'

He looked at her suspiciously, his mind questioning: Is it a trick? He hid the movement of his throat in swallowing coffee. It was stupid, he thought, to be so suspicious.

He put down the cup.

'Good,' he said. 'Very good.'

He looked at her as she stared into the coffee.

'If you *are* infected,' he told her, 'I'll do everything I can to cure you.'

Her eyes met his. 'And if you can't?' she said.

Silence a moment.

'Let's wait and see,' he said then.

They both drank coffee. Then he asked, 'Shall we do it now?'

'Please,' she said, 'in the morning. I . . . still feel a little ill.'

'All right,' he said, nodding. 'In the morning.'

They finished their meal in silence. Neville felt only a small satisfaction that she was going to let him check her blood. He was afraid he might discover that she *was* infected. In the meantime he had to pass an evening and a night with her, perhaps get to know her and be attracted to her. When in the morning he might have to . . .

Later, in the living room, they sat looking at the mural, sipping port, and listening to Schubert's Fourth Symphony.

'I wouldn't have believed it,' she said, seeming to cheer up. 'I never thought I'd be listening to music again. Drinking wine.'

She looked around the room.

'You've certainly done a wonderful job,' she said.

'What about *your* house?' he asked.

'It was nothing like this,' she said. 'We didn't have a—'

'How did you protect your house?' he interrupted.

'Oh—' She thought a moment. 'We had it boarded up, of course. And we used crosses.'

'They don't always work,' he said quietly, after a moment of looking at her.

She looked blank. 'They don't?'

'Why should a Jew fear the cross?' he said. 'Why should a vampire who had been a Jew fear it? Most people were afraid of becoming vampires. Most of them suffer from hysterical blindness before mirrors. But as far as the cross goes – well, neither a Jew nor a Hindu nor a Mohammedan nor an atheist, for that matter, would fear the cross.'

She sat holding her wineglass and looking at him with expressionless eyes.

'That's why the cross doesn't always work,' he said.

'You didn't let me finish,' she said. 'We used garlic too.'

'I thought it made you sick.'

'I was already sick. I used to weigh a hundred and twenty. I weigh ninety-eight pounds now.'

He nodded. But as he went into the kitchen to get another bottle of wine he thought she would have adjusted to it by now. After three years.

Then again, she might not have. What was the point in doubting her now? She was going to let him check her blood. What else could she do? It's me, he thought. I've been by myself too long. I won't believe anything unless I see it in a microscope. Heredity triumphs again. I'm my father's son, damn his moldering bones.

Standing in the dark kitchen, digging his blunt nail under

the wrapping around the neck of the bottle, Robert Neville looked into the living room at Ruth.

His eyes ran over the robe, resting a moment on the slight prominence of her breasts, dropping then to the bronzed calves and ankles, up to the smooth kneecaps. She had a body like a young girl's. She certainly didn't look like the mother of two.

The most unusual feature of the entire affair, he thought, was that he felt no physical desire for her.

If she had come two years before, maybe even later, he might have violated her. There had been some terrible moments in those days, moments when the most terrible of solutions to his need were considered, were often dwelt upon until they drove him half mad.

But then the experiments had begun. Smoking had tapered off, drinking lost its compulsive nature. Deliberately and with surprising success, he had submerged himself in investigation.

His sex drive had diminished, had virtually disappeared. Salvation of the monk, he thought. The drive had to go sooner or later, or no normal man could dedicate himself to any life that excluded sex.

Now, happily, he felt almost nothing; perhaps a hardly discernible stirring far beneath the rocky strata of abstinence. He was content to leave it at that. Especially since there was no certainty that Ruth was the companion he had waited for. Or even the certainty that he could allow her to live beyond tomorrow. *Cure* her?

Curing was unlikely.

He went back into the living room with the opened bottle. She smiled at him briefly as he poured more wine for her.

'I've been admiring your mural,' she said. 'It almost makes you believe you're in the woods.'

He grunted.

'It must have taken a lot of work to get your house like this,' she said.

'You should know,' he said. 'You went through the same thing.'

'We had nothing like this,' she said. 'Our house was small. Our food locker was half the size of yours.'

'You must have run out of food,' he said, looking at her carefully.

'Frozen food,' she said. 'We were living out of cans.'

He nodded. Logical, his mind had to admit. But he still didn't like it. It was all intuition, he knew, but he didn't like it.

'What about water?' he asked then.

She looked at him silently for a moment.

'You don't believe a word I've said, do you?' she said.

'It's not that,' he said. 'I'm just curious how you lived.'

'You can't hide it from your voice,' she said. 'You've been alone too long. You've lost the talent for deceit.'

He grunted, getting the uncomfortable feeling that she was playing with him. That's ridiculous, he argued. She's just a woman. She was probably right. He probably *was* a gruff and graceless hermit. What did it matter?

'Tell me about your husband,' he said abruptly.

Something flitted over her face, a shade of memory. She lifted the glass of dark wine to her lips.

'Not now,' she said. 'Please.'

He slumped back on the couch, unable to analyze the formless dissatisfaction he felt. Everything she said and did could be a result of what she'd been through. It could also be a lie.

Why should she lie? he asked himself. In the morning he would check her blood. What could lying tonight profit her when, in a matter of hours, he'd know the truth?

'You know,' he said, trying to ease the moment, 'I've been thinking. If three people could survive the plague, why not more?'

'Do you think that's possible?' she asked.

'Why not? There must have been others who were immune for one reason or another.'

'Tell me more about the germ,' she said.

He hesitated a moment, then put down his wineglass. What if he told her everything? What if she escaped and came back after death with all the knowledge that *he* had?

'There's an awful lot of detail,' he said.

126

'You were saying something about the cross before,' she said. 'How do you know it's true?'

'You remember what I said about Ben Cortman?' he said, glad to restate something she already knew rather than go into fresh material.

'You mean that man you—'

He nodded. 'Yes. Come here,' he said, standing. 'I'll show him to you.'

As he stood behind her looking out the peephole, he smelled the odor of her hair and skin. It made him draw back a little. Isn't that remarkable? he thought. I don't like the smell. Like Gulliver returning from the logical horses, I find the human smell offensive.

'He's the one by the lamppost,' he said.

She made a slight sound of acknowledgment. Then she said, 'There are so few. Where are they?'

'I've killed off most of them,' he said, 'but they manage to keep a few ahead of me.'

'How come the lamp is on out there?' she said. 'I thought they destroyed the electrical system.'

'I connected it with my generator,' he said, 'so I could watch them.'

'Don't they break the bulb?'

'I have a very strong globe over the bulb.'

'Don't they climb up and try to break it?'

'I have garlic all over the post.'

She shook her head. 'You've thought of everything.'

Stepping back, he looked at her a moment. How can she look at them so calmly, he wondered, ask me questions, make comments, when only a week ago she saw their kind tear her husband to pieces? Doubts again, he thought. Won't they ever stop?

He knew they wouldn't until he knew about her for sure.

She turned away from the window then.

'Will you excuse me a moment?' she said.

He watched her walk into the bathroom and heard her lock the door behind her. Then he went back to the couch after closing the peephole door. A wry smile played on his lips. He looked down into the tawny wine depths and tugged abstractedly at his beard.

'Will you excuse me a moment?'

For some reason the words seemed grotesquely amusing, the carry-over from a lost age. Emily Post mincing through the graveyard. Etiquette for Young Vampires.

The smile was gone.

And what now? What did the future hold for him? In a week would she still be here with him, or crumpled in the never-cooling fire?

He knew that, if she were infected, he'd have to try to cure her whether it worked or not. But what if she were free of the bacillus? In a way, that was a more nerve-racking possibility. The other way he would merely go on as before, breaking neither schedule nor standards. But if she stayed, if they had to establish a relationship, perhaps become husband and wife, have children . . .

Yes, that was more terrifying.

He suddenly realized that he had become an ill-tempered and inveterate bachelor again. He no longer thought about his wife, his child, his past life. The present was enough. And he was afraid of the possible demand that he make sacrifices and accept responsibility again. He was afraid of giving out his heart, of removing the chains he had forged around it to keep emotion prisoner. He was afraid of loving again.

When she came out of the bathroom he was still sitting there, thinking. The record player, unnoticed by him, let out only a thin scratching sound.

Ruth lifted the record from the turntable and turned it. The third movement of the symphony began.

'Well, what about Cortman?' she asked, sitting down.

He looked at her blankly. 'Cortman?'

'You were going to tell me something about him and the cross.'

'Oh. Well, one night I got him in here and showed him the cross.'

'What happened?'

Shall I kill her now? Shall I not even investigate, but kill her and burn her?

His throat moved. Such thoughts were a hideous testimony to the world he had accepted; a world in which murder was easier than hope.

Well, he wasn't that far gone yet, he thought. I'm a man, not a destroyer.

'What's wrong?' she said nervously.

'What?'

'You're staring at me.'

'I'm sorry,' he said coldly. 'I . . . I'm just thinking.'

She didn't say any more. She drank her wine and he saw her hand shake as she held the glass. He forced down all introspection. He didn't want her to know what he felt.

'When I showed him the cross,' he said, 'he laughed in my face.'

She nodded once.

'But when I held a torah before his eyes, I got the reaction I wanted.'

'A what?'

'A torah. Tablet of law, I believe it is.'

'And that . . . got a reaction?'

'Yes. I had him tied up, but when he saw the torah he broke loose and attacked me.'

'What happened?' She seemed to have lost her fright again.

'He struck me on the head with something. I don't remember what. I was almost knocked out. But, using the torah, I backed him to the door and got rid of him.'

'Oh.'

'So you see, the cross hasn't the power the legend says it has. My theory is that, since the legend came into its own in Europe, a continent predominantly Catholic, the cross would naturally become the symbol of defense against powers of darkness.'

'Couldn't you use your gun on Cortman?' she asked.

'How do you know I had a gun?'

'I . . . assumed as much,' she said. '*We* had guns.'

'Then you must know bullets have no effect on vampires.'

'We were . . . never sure,' she said, then went on quickly: 'Do you know why that's so? Why don't bullets affect them?'

He shook his head. 'I don't know,' he said.

They sat in silence listening to the music.

He did know, but, doubting again, he didn't want to tell her.

Through experiments on the dead vampires he had discovered that the bacilli effected the creation of a powerful body glue that sealed bullet openings as soon as they were made. Bullets were enclosed almost immediately, and since the system was activated by germs, a bullet couldn't hurt it. The system could, in fact, contain almost an indefinite amount of bullets, since the body glue prevented a penetration of more than a few fractions of an inch. Shooting vampires was like throwing pebbles into tar.

As he sat looking at her, she arranged the folds of the robe around her legs and he got a momentary glimpse of brown thigh. Far from being attracted, he felt irritated. It was a typical feminine gesture, he thought, an artificial movement.

As the moments passed he could almost sense himself drifting farther and farther from her. In a way he almost regretted having found her at all. Through the years he had achieved a certain degree of peace. He had accepted solitude, found it not half bad. Now this . . . ending it all.

In order to fill the emptiness of the moment, he reached for his pipe and pouch. He stuffed tobacco into the bowl and lit it. For a second he wondered if he should ask if she minded. He didn't ask.

The music ended. She got up and he watched her while she looked through his records. She seemed like a young girl, she was so slender. Who is she? he thought. Who is she really?

'May I play this?' she asked, holding up an album.

He didn't even look at it. 'If you like,' he said.

She sat down as Rachmaninoff's Second Piano Concerto

began. Her taste isn't remarkably advanced, he thought, looking at her without expression.

'Tell me about yourself,' she said.

Another typical feminine question, he thought. Then he berated himself for being so critical. What was the point in irritating himself by doubting her?

'Nothing to tell,' he said.

She was smiling again. *Was* she laughing at him?

'You scared the life out of me this afternoon,' she said. 'You and your bristly beard. And those wild eyes.'

He blew out smoke. Wild eyes? That was ridiculous.

What was she trying to do? Break down his reserve with cuteness?

'What do you look like under all those whiskers?' she asked.

He tried to smile at her but he couldn't.

'Nothing,' he said. 'Just an ordinary face.'

'How old are you, Robert?'

His throat moved. It was the first time she'd spoken his name. It gave him a strange, restless feeling to hear a woman speak his name after so long. Don't call me that, he almost said to her. He didn't want to lose the distance between them. If she were infected and he couldn't cure her, he wanted it to be a stranger that he put away.

She turned her head away.

'You don't have to talk to me if you don't want to,' she said quietly. 'I won't bother you. I'll go tomorrow.'

His chest muscles tightened.

'But . . .' he said.

'I don't want to spoil your life,' she said. 'You don't have to feel any obligation to me just because . . . we're the only ones left.'

His eyes were bleak as he looked at her, and he felt a brief stirring of guilt at her words. Why should I doubt her? he told himself. If she's infected, she'll never get away alive. What's there to fear?

'I'm sorry,' he said. 'I . . . I *have* been alone a long time.'

She didn't look up.

'If you'd like to talk,' he said, 'I'll be glad to . . . tell you anything I can.'

She hesitated a moment. Then she looked at him, her eyes not committing themselves at all.

'I *would* like to know about the disease,' she said. 'I lost my two girls because of it. And it caused my husband's death.'

He looked at her and then spoke.

'It's a bacillus,' he said, 'a cylindrical bacterium. It creates an isotonic solution in the blood, circulates the blood slower than normal, activates all bodily functions, lives on fresh blood, and provides energy. Deprived of blood, it makes self-killing bacteriophages or else sporulates.'

She looked blank. He realized then that she couldn't have understood. Terms so common to him now were completely foreign to her.

'Well,' he said, 'most of those things aren't so important. To sporulate is to create an oval body that has all the basic ingredients of the vegetative bacterium. The germ does that when it gets no fresh blood. Then, when the vampire host decomposes, these spores go flying out and seek new hosts. They find one, germinate – and one more system is infected.'

She shook her head incredulously.

'Bacteriophages are inanimate proteins that are also created when the system gets no blood. Unlike the spores, though, in this case abnormal metabolism destroys the cells.'

Quickly he told her about the imperfect waste disposal of the lymphatic system, the garlic as allergen causing anaphylaxis, the various vectors of the disease.

'Then why are we immune?' she asked.

For a long moment he looked at her, withholding any answer. Then, with a shrug, he said, 'I don't know about you. As for me, while I was stationed in Panama during the war I was bitten by a vampire bat. And, though I can't prove it, my theory is that the bat had previously encountered a true vampire and acquired the *vampiris* germ. The germ caused the bat to seek human rather than animal blood. But, by the time the germ had passed into my system, it had been weakened in some way by the bat's system. It made me terribly ill, of course, but it didn't kill me, and as a result, my body built up an immunity to it. That's my theory, anyway. I can't find any better reason.'

'But . . . didn't the same thing happen to others down there?'

'I don't know,' he said quietly. 'I killed the bat.' He shrugged. 'Maybe I was the first human it had attacked.'

She looked at him without a word, her surveillance making Neville feel restive. He went on talking even though he didn't really want to.

Briefly he told her about the major obstacle in his study of the vampires.

'At first I thought the stake had to hit their hearts,' he said. 'I believed the legend. I found out that wasn't so. I put stakes in all parts of their bodies and they died. That made me think it was hemorrhage. But then one day . . .'

And he told her about the woman who had decomposed before his eyes.

'I knew then it couldn't be hemorrhage,' he went on, feeling a sort of pleasure in reciting his discoveries. 'I didn't know what to do. Then one day it came to me.'

'What?' she asked.

'I took a dead vampire. I put his arm into an artificial vacuum. I punctured his arm inside that vacuum. Blood spurted out.' He paused. 'But that's all.'

She stared at him.

'You don't see,' he said.

'I . . . No,' she admitted.

'When I let air back into the tank, the arm decomposed,' he said.

She still stared.

'You see,' he said, 'the bacillus is a facultative saprophyte. It lives with or without oxygen; but with a difference. Inside the system, it is anaerobic and sets up a symbiosis with the system.

The vampire feeds it fresh blood, the bacteria provides the energy so the vampire can get more fresh blood. The germ also causes, I might add, the growth of the canine teeth.'

'Yes?' she said.

'When air enters,' he said, 'the situation changes instantaneously. The germ becomes aerobic and, instead of being symbiotic, it becomes virulently parasitic.' He paused. 'It eats the host,' he said.

'Then the stake . . .' she started.

'Lets air in. Of course. Lets it in and keeps the flesh open so that the body glue can't function. So the heart has nothing to do with it. What I do now is cut the wrists deep enough so that the body glue can't work.' He smiled a little. 'When I think of all the time I used to spend making stakes!'

She nodded and, noticing the wineglass in her hand, put it down.

'That's why the woman I told you about broke down so rapidly,' he said. 'She'd been dead so long that as soon as air struck her system the germs caused spontaneous dissolution.'

Her throat moved and a shudder ran down through her.

'It's horrible,' she said.

He looked at her in surprise. Horrible? Wasn't that odd? He hadn't thought that for years. For him the word horror had become obsolete. A surfeiting of terror soon made terror a cliché. To Robert Neville the situation merely existed as natural fact. It had no adjectives.

'And what about the . . . the ones who are still alive?' she asked.

'Well,' he said, 'when you cut their wrists the germ naturally becomes parasitic. But mostly they die from simple hemorrhage.'

'*Simple*—'

She turned away quickly and her lips were pressed into a tight, thin line.

'What's the matter?' he asked.

'N-nothing. Nothing,' she said.

He smiled. 'One gets used to these things,' he said. 'One has to.'

Again she shuddered, the smooth column of her throat contracting.

'You can't abide by Robert's Rules of Order in the jungle,' he said. 'Believe me, it's the only thing I can do. Is it better to let them die of the disease and return – in a far more terrible way?'

She pressed her hands together.

'But you said a lot of them are – are still living,' she said nervously. 'How do you know they're not going to *stay* alive?'

'I know,' he said. 'I know the germ, know how it multiplies. No matter how long their systems fight it, in the end the germ will win. I've made antibiotics, injected dozens of them. But it doesn't work, it can't work. You can't make vaccines work when they're already deep in the disease. Their bodies can't fight germs and make antibodies at the same time. It can't be done, believe me. It's a trap. If I didn't kill them, sooner or later they'd die and come after me. I have no choice; no choice at all.'

They were silent then and the only sound in the room was the rasping of the needle on the inner grooves of the record. She wouldn't look at him, but kept staring at the floor with bleak eyes. It was strange, he thought, to find himself vaguely on the defensive for what yesterday was accepted necessity. In the years that had passed he had never once considered the possibility that he was wrong. It took her presence to bring about such thoughts. And they were strange, alien thoughts.

'Do you actually think I'm wrong?' he asked in an incredulous voice.

She bit into her lower lip.

'Ruth,' he said.

'It's not for me to say,' she answered.

CHAPTER EIGHTEEN

'Virge!'

The dark form recoiled against the wall as Robert Neville's hoarse cry ripped open the silent blackness.

He jerked his body up from the couch and stared with sleep-clouded eyes across the room, his chest pulsing with heartbeats like maniac fists on a dungeon wall.

He lurched up to his feet, brain still foggy with sleep, unable to define time or place.

'Virge?' he said again, weakly, shakily. 'Virge?'

'It – it's me,' the faltering voice said in the darkness. He took a trembling step toward the thin stream of light spearing through the open peephole. He blinked dully at the light.

She gasped as he put his hand out and clutched her shoulder.

'It's Ruth. *Ruth*,' she said in a terrified whisper.

He stood there rocking slowly in the darkness, eyes gazing without comprehension at the dark form before him.

'It's Ruth,' she said again, more loudly.

Waking came like a hose blast of numbing shock. Something twisted cold knots into his chest and stomach. It wasn't Virge. He shook his head suddenly, rubbed shaking fingers across his eyes.

Then he stood there staring, weighted beneath a sudden depression.

'Oh,' he muttered faintly. 'Oh, I . . .'

He remained there, feeling his body weaving slowly in the dark as the mists cleared from his brain.

He looked at the open peephole, then back at her.

'What are you doing?' he asked, voice still thick with sleep.

'Nothing,' she said nervously. 'I . . . couldn't sleep.'

He blinked his eyes suddenly at the flaring lamplight. Then his hands dropped down from the lamp switch and he turned around. She was against the wall still, blinking at the light, her hands at her sides drawn into tight fists.

'Why are you dressed?' he asked in a surprised voice.

Her throat moved and she stared at him. He rubbed his eyes again and pushed back the long hair from his temples.

'I was . . . just looking out,' she said.

'But why are you dressed?'

'I couldn't sleep.'

He stood looking at her, still a little groggy, feeling his heartbeat slowly diminish. Through the open peephole he heard them yelling outside, and he heard Cortman shout, 'Come out, Neville!' Moving to the peephole, he pushed the small wooden door shut and turned to her.

'I want to know why you're dressed,' he said again.

'No reason,' she said.

'Were you going to leave while I was asleep?'

'No, I . . .'

'*Were* you?'

She gasped as he grabbed her wrist.

'No, no,' she said quickly. 'How could I, with them out there?'

He stood breathing heavily, looking at her frightened face. His throat moved slowly as he remembered the shock of waking up and thinking that she was Virge.

Abruptly he dropped her arm and turned away. And he'd thought the past was dead. How long did it take for a past to die?

She said nothing as he poured a tumblerful of whisky and

swallowed it convulsively. Virge, Virge, he thought miserably, still with me. He closed his eyes and jammed his teeth together.

'Was that her name?' he heard Ruth ask.

His muscles tightened, then went slack.

'It's all right,' he said in a dead voice. 'Go to bed.'

She drew back a little. 'I'm sorry,' she said. 'I didn't mean . . .'

Suddenly he knew he didn't want her to go to bed. He wanted her to stay with him. He didn't know why, he just didn't want to be alone.

'I thought you were my wife,' he heard himself saying. 'I woke up and I thought—'

He drank a mouthful of whisky, coughing as part of it went down the wrong way. Ruth stayed in the shadows, listening.

'She came back, you see,' he said. 'I buried her, but one night she came back. She looked like – like you did. An outline, a shadow. *Dead*. But she came back. I tried to keep her with me. I tried, but she wasn't the same any more . . . you see. All she wanted was—'

He forced down the sob in his throat.

'My own wife,' he said in a trembling voice, 'coming back to drink my blood!'

He jammed down the glass on the bar top. Turning away, he paced restlessly to the peephole, turned, and went back and stood again before the bar. Ruth said nothing; she just stood in the darkness, listening.

'I put her away again,' he said. 'I had to do the same thing to her I'd done to the others. My own wife.' There was a clicking in his throat. 'A stake,' he said in a terrible voice. 'I had to put a stake in her. It was the only thing I knew to do. I—'

He couldn't finish. He stood there a long time, shivering helplessly, his eyes tightly shut.

Then he spoke again.

'Almost three years ago I did that. And I still remember it, it's still with me. What can you do? What can you *do*?' He drove a fist down on the bar top as the anguish of memory

138

swept over him again. 'No matter how you try, you can't forget or – or adjust or – *ever* get away from it!'

He ran shaking fingers through his hair.

'I know what you feel, I know. I didn't at first, I didn't trust you. I was safe, secure in my little shell. Now . . .' He shook his head slowly, defeatedly. 'In a second, it's all gone. Adjustment, security, peace – all gone.'

'Robert.'

Her voice was as broken and lost as his.

'Why were we punished like this?' she asked.

He drew in a shuddering breath.

'I don't know,' he answered bitterly. 'There's no answer, no reason. It just is.'

She was close to him now. And suddenly, without hesitation or drawing back, he drew her against him, and they were two people holding each other tightly in the lost measure of night.

'Robert, *Robert.*'

Her hands rubbed over his back, stroking and clutching, while his arms held her firmly and he pressed his eyes shut against her warm, soft hair.

Their mouths held together for a long time and her arms gripped with desperate tightness around his neck.

Then they were sitting in the darkness, pressing close to-gether, as if all the heat in the world were in their bodies and they would share the warmth between them. He felt the shuddering rise and fall of her breasts as she held close to him, her arms tight around his body, her face against his neck. His big hands moved roughly through her hair, stroking and feeling the silky strands.

'I'm sorry, Ruth.'

'Sorry?'

'For being so cruel to you, for not trusting you.'

She was silent, holding tight.

'Oh, Robert,' she said then, 'it's so unfair. So *unfair*. Why are we still alive? Why aren't we all dead? It would be better if we were all dead.'

'Shhh, shhh,' he said, feeling emotion for her like a released current pouring from his heart and mind. 'It'll be all right.'

He felt her shaking her head slowly against him.

'It will, it will,' he said.

'How can it?'

'It *will*,' he said, even though he knew he really couldn't believe it, even though he knew it was only released tension forming words in his mind.

'No,' she said. 'No.'

'Yes, it will. It will, Ruth.'

He didn't know how long it was they sat there holding each other close. He forgot everything, time and place; it was just the two of them together, needing each other, survivors of a black terror embracing because they had found each other.

But then he wanted to do something for her, to help her.

'Come,' he said. 'We'll check you.'

She stiffened in his arms.

'No, no,' he said quickly. 'Don't be afraid. I'm sure we won't find anything. But if we do, I'll cure you. I swear I'll cure you, Ruth.'

She was looking at him in the darkness, not saying a word. He stood and pulled her up with him, trembling with an excitement he hadn't felt in endless years. He wanted to cure her, to help her.

'Let me,' he said. 'I won't hurt you. I promise I won't. Let's *know*. Let's find out for sure. Then we can plan and work. I'll save you, Ruth. I will. Or I'll die myself.'

She was still tense, holding back.

'Come with me, Ruth.'

Now that the strength of his reserve had gone, there was nothing left to brace himself on, and he was shaking like a palsied man.

He led her into the bedroom. And when he saw in the lamplight how frightened she was, he pulled her close and stroked her hair.

'It's all right,' he said. 'All right, Ruth. No matter what we find, it'll be all right. Don't you understand?'

He sat her down on the stool and her face was completely blank, her body shuddering as he heated the needle over a Bunsen flame.

He bent over and kissed her on the cheek.

'It's all right now,' he said gently. 'It's all right.'

She closed her eyes as he jabbed in the needle. He could feel the pain in his own finger as he pressed out blood and rubbed it on the slide.

'There. There,' he said anxiously, pressing a little cotton to the nick on her finger. He felt himself trembling helplessly. No matter how he tried to control it, he couldn't. His fingers were almost incapable of making the slide, and he kept looking at Ruth and smiling at her, trying to take the look of taut fright from her features.

'Don't be afraid,' he said. 'Please don't. I'll cure you if you're infected. I will Ruth, I will.'

She sat without a word, looking at him with listless eyes as he worked. Her hands kept stirring restlessly in her lap.

'What will you do if – if I *am*?' she said then.

'I'm not sure,' he said. 'Not yet. But there are a lot of things we can do.'

'What?'

'Vaccines, for one.'

'You said vaccines didn't work,' she said, her voice shaking a little.

'Yes, but . . .' He broke off as he slid the glass slide onto the microscope.

'Robert, what could you do?'

She slid off the stool as he bent over the microscope.

'Robert, don't look!' she begged suddenly, her voice pleading.

But he'd already seen.

He didn't realize that his breath had stopped. His blank eyes met hers.

'Ruth,' he whispered in a shocked voice.

The wooden mallet crashed down on his forehead.

A burst of pain filled Robert Neville's head and he felt one leg give way. As he fell to one side he knocked over the microscope. His right knee hit the floor and he looked up in dazed bewilderment at her fright-twisted face. The mallet came down again and he cried out in pain. He fell to both knees and his palms struck the floor as he toppled forward. A hundred miles away he heard her gasping sob.

'Ruth,' he mumbled.

'I *told* you not to!' she cried.

He clutched out at her legs and she drove the mallet down a third time, this time on the back of his skull.

'*Ruth!*'

Robert Neville's hands went limp and slid off her calves, rubbing away part of the tan. He fell on his face and his fingers drew in convulsively as night filled his brain.

CHAPTER NINETEEN

When he opened his eyes there was no sound in the house.

He lay there a moment looking confusedly at the floor. Then, with a startled grunt, he sat up. A package of needles exploded in his head and he slumped down on the cold floor, hands pressed to his throbbing skull. A clicking sound filled his throat as he lay there.

After a few minutes he pulled himself up slowly by gripping the edge of the bench. The floor undulated beneath him as he held on tightly, eyes closed, legs wavering.

A minute later he managed to stumble into the bathroom. There he threw cold water in his face and sat on the bathtub edge pressing a cold, wet cloth to his forehead.

What had happened? He kept blinking and staring at the white-tiled floor.

He stood up and walked slowly into the living room. It was empty. The front door stood half open in the gray of early morning. She was gone.

Then he remembered. He struggled back to the bedroom, using the walls to guide him.

The note was on the bench next to the overturned microscope. He picked up the paper with numbed fingers and carried it to the bed. Sinking down with a groan, he held the letter before his eyes. But the letters blurred and ran. He shook his head and pressed his eyes shut. After a little while he read:

Robert:

Now you know. Know that I was spying on you, know that almost everything I told you was a lie.

I'm writing this note, though, because I want to save you if I can.

When I was first given the job of spying on you, I had no feelings about your life. Because I *did* have a husband, Robert. You killed him.

But now it's different. I know now that you were just as much forced into your situation as we were forced into ours. We *are* infected. But you already know that. What you don't understand yet is that we're going to stay alive. We've found a way to do that and we're going to set up society again slowly but surely. We're going to do away with all those wretched creatures whom death has cheated. And, even though I pray otherwise, we may decide to kill you and those like you.

Those like me? he thought with a start. But he kept reading.

I'll try to save you. I'll tell them you're too well armed for us to attack now. Use the time I'm giving you, Robert! Get away from your house, go into the mountains and save yourself. There are only a handful of us now. But sooner or later we'll be too well organized, and nothing I say will stop the rest from destroying you. For God's sake, Robert, go now, while you can!

I know you may not believe this. You may not believe that we can live in the sun for short periods now. You may not believe that my tan was only make-up. You may not believe that we can live with the germ now.

That's why I'm leaving one of my pills.

I took them all the time I was here. I kept them in a belt around my waist. You'll discover that they're a combination of defebrinated blood and a drug. I don't know myself just what it is. The blood feeds the germs, the drug prevents its

144

multiplication. It was the discovery of this pill that saved us from dying, that is helping to set up society again slowly. Believe me, it's true. And escape!

Forgive me, too. I didn't mean to hit you, it nearly killed me to do it. But I was so terribly frightened of what you'd do when you found out.

Forgive me for having to lie to you about so many things. But please believe this: When we were together in the darkness, close to each other, I wasn't spying on you. I was loving you.

RUTH

He read the letter again. Then his hands fell forward and he sat there staring with empty eyes at the floor. He couldn't believe it. He shook his head slowly and tried to understand, but adjustment eluded him.

He walked unsteadily to the bench. He picked up the small amber pill and held it in his palm, smelled it, tasted it. He felt as if all the security of reason were ebbing away from him. The framework of his life was collapsing and it frightened him.

Yet how did he refute the evidence? The pill, the tan coming off her leg, her walking in the sun, her reaction to garlic.

He sank down on the stool and looked at the mallet lying on the floor. Slowly, ploddingly, his mind went over the evidence.

When he'd first seen her she'd run from him. Had it been a ruse? No, she'd been genuinely frightened. She must have been startled by his cry, then, even though she'd been expecting it, and forgotten all about her job. Then later, when she'd calmed down, she'd talked him into thinking that her reaction to garlic was the reaction of a sick stomach. And she had lied and smiled and feigned hopeless acceptance and carefully got all the information she'd been sent after. And, when she'd wanted to leave, she couldn't because of Cortman and the others. He had awakened then. They had embraced, they had . . .

His white-knuckled fist jolted down on the bench. 'I was

loving you.' Lie. Lie! His fingers crumpled up the letter and flung it away bitterly.

Rage made the pain in his head flare hotly and he pressed both hands against it and closed his eyes with a groan.

Then he looked up. Slowly he slid off the stool and placed the microscope back on its base.

The rest of her letter wasn't a lie, he knew that. Without the pill, without any evidence of word or memory, he knew. He knew what even Ruth and her people didn't seem to know.

He looked into the eyepiece for a long time. Yes, he knew. And the admission of what he saw changed his entire world. How stupid and ineffective he felt for never having foreseen it! Especially after reading the phrase a hundred, a thousand times. But then he'd never really appreciated it. Such a short phrase it was, but meaning so much.

Bacteria can mutate.

PART 4: JANUARY 1979

CHAPTER TWENTY

They came by night. Came in their dark cars with their spotlights and their guns and their axes and pikes. Came from the blackness with a great sound of motors, the long white arms of their spotlights snapping around the boulevard corner and clutching out at Cimarron Street.

Robert Neville was sitting at the peephole when they came. He had put down a book and was sitting there watching idly when the beams splashed white across the bloodless vampire faces and they whirled with a gasp, their dark animal eyes staring at the blinding lights.

Neville jumped back from the peephole, his heart thudding with the abrupt shock. For a moment he stood there trembling in the dark room, unable to decide what to do. His throat contracted and he heard the roar of the car motors even through the soundproofing on his house. He thought of the pistols in his bureau, the sub-machine gun on his workbench, thought of defending his house against them.

Then he pressed his fingers in until the nails dug at his palms. No, he'd made his decision, he'd worked it out carefully through the past months. He would not fight.

With a heavy, sinking sensation in the pit of his stomach he stepped back to the peephole and looked out.

The street was a scene of rushing, violent action illuminated by the bald glare of the spotlights. Men rushed at men, the sound of running boots covered the pavement. Then a shot rang out, echoing hollowly; more shots.

Two male vampires went thrashing down onto their sides. Four men grabbed them by the arms and jerked them up while two other men drove the glittering lance points of their pikes into the vampires' chests. Neville's face twitched as screams filled the night. He felt his chest shuddering with labored breath as he watched from his house.

The dark-suited men knew exactly what they were doing. There were about seven vampires visible, six men and a woman. The men surrounded the seven, held their flailing arms, and drove razor-tipped pikes deep into their bodies. Blood spouted out on the dark pavement and the vampires perished one by one. Neville felt himself shivering more and more. Is this the new society? The words flashed across his mind. He tried to believe that the men were forced into what they were doing, but shock brought terrible doubt. Did they have to do it like this, with such a black and brutal slaughtering? Why did they slay with alarum by night, when by day the vampires could be dispatched in peace?

Robert Neville felt tight fists shaking at his sides. He didn't like the looks of them, he didn't like the methodical butchery. They were more like gangsters than men forced into a situation. There were looks of vicious triumph on their faces, white and stark in the spotlights. Their faces were cruel and emotionless.

Suddenly Neville felt himself shudder violently, remembering. Where was Ben Cortman?

His eyes fled over the street but he couldn't see Cortman. He pressed against the peephole and looked up and down the street. He didn't want them to get Cortman, he realized, didn't want them to destroy Cortman like that. With a sense of inward shock he could not analyze in the rush of the moment, he realized that he felt more deeply toward the vampires than he did toward their executioners.

Now the seven vampires lay crumpled and still in their pools of stolen blood. The spotlights were moving around the street, flaying open the night. Neville turned his head away as the brilliant glare blazed across the front of his house. Then the spotlight had turned about and he looked again.

A shout. Neville's eyes jumped toward the focus of the spotlights.

He stiffened.

Cortman was on the roof of the house across the street. He was pulling himself up toward the chimney, body flattened on the shingles.

Abruptly it came to Neville that it was in that chimney that Ben Cortman had hidden most of the time, and he felt a wrench of despair at the knowledge. His lips pressed together tightly. Why hadn't he looked more carefully? He couldn't fight the sick apprehension he felt at the thought of Cortman being killed by these brutal strangers. Objectively, it was pointless, but he could not repress the feeling. Cortman was not theirs to put to rest.

But there was nothing he could do.

With bleak, tortured eyes he watched the spotlights cluster on Cortman's wriggling body. He watched the white hands reaching out slowly for handholds on the roof. Slowly, slowly, as if Cortman had all the time in the world. Hurry up! Neville felt himself twitch with the unspoken words as he watched. He felt himself straining with Cortman's agonizingly slow movements.

The men did not shout, they did not command. They raised their rifles now and the night was torn open again with their exploding fire.

Neville almost felt the bullets in his own flesh. His body jerked with convulsive shudders as he watched Cortman's body jerk under the impact of the bullets.

Still Cortman kept crawling, and Neville saw his white face, his teeth gritted together. The end of Oliver Hardy, he thought, the death of all comedy and all laughter. He didn't hear the continuous fusillade of shots. He didn't even feel the tears running down his cheeks. His eyes were riveted on the ungainly form of his old friend inching up the brightly lit roof.

Now Cortman rose up on his knees and clutched at the chimney edge with spasmodic fingers. His body lurched as more bullets struck. His dark eyes glared into the blinding spotlights, his lips were drawn back in a soundless snarl.

Then he was standing up beside the chimney and Neville's face was white and taut as he watched Cortman start to raise his right leg.

And then the hammering machine gun splattered Cortman's flesh with lead. For a moment Cortman stood erect in the hot blast, palsied hands raised high over his head, a look of berserk defiance twisting his white features.

'Ben,' Neville muttered in a croaking whisper.

Ben Cortman's body folded, slumped forward, fell. It slid and rolled slowly down the shingled incline, then dropped into space. In the sudden silence Neville heard the thump of it from across the street. Sick-eyed, he watched the men rush at the writhing body with their pikes.

Then Neville closed his eyes and his nails dug furrows in the flesh of his palms.

A clumping of boots. Neville jerked back into the darkness. He stood in the middle of the room, waiting for them to call to him and tell him to come out. He held himself rigidly. I'm not going to fight, he told himself strongly. Even though he wanted to fight, even though he already hated the dark men with their guns and their bloodstained pikes.

But he wasn't going to fight. He had worked out his decision very carefully. They were doing what they had to do, albeit with unnecessary violence and seeming relish. He had killed their people and they had to capture him and save themselves. He would not fight. He'd throw himself upon the justice of their new society. When they called to him he would go out and surrender; it was his decision.

But they didn't call. Neville lurched back with a gasp as the ax blade bit deeply into the front door. He stood trembling in the dark living room. What were they doing? Why didn't they call on him to surrender? He wasn't a vampire, he was a man like them. What were they doing?

He whirled and stared at the kitchen. They were chopping at the boarded-up back door too. He took a nervous step toward the hallway. His frightened eyes rushed from the back to the front door. He felt his heart pumping. He didn't understand, he didn't understand!

With a grunt of shocked surprise he jumped into the hall as the enclosed house rang with the gun explosion. The men were shooting away the lock on the front door. Another reverberating shot made his ears ring.

And, suddenly, he knew. They weren't going to take him to their courts, to their justice. They were going to exterminate him.

With a frightened murmur he ran into the bedroom. His hands fumbled in the bureau drawer.

He straightened up on trembling legs, the guns in his hands. But what if they *were* going to take him prisoner? He'd only judged by the fact that they hadn't called on him to come out. There were no lights in the house; maybe they thought he was already gone.

He stood shivering in the darkness of the bedroom, not knowing what to do, mutters of terror filling his throat. Why hadn't he left! Why hadn't he listened to her and left? Fool!

One of his guns fell from nerveless fingers as the front door was crushed in. Heavy feet thudded into the living room and Robert Neville shuffled back across the floor, his remaining pistol held out with rigid, blood-drained fingers. They weren't going to kill him without a fight!

He gasped as he collided with the bench. He stood there tautly. In the front room a man said something he couldn't understand, then flashlight beams shone into the hall. Neville caught his breath. He felt the room spinning around him. So this is the end. It was the only thing he could think. So this is the end.

Heavy shoes thumped in the hall. Neville's fingers tightened still more on the pistol and his eyes stared with wild fright at the doorway.

Two men came in.

Their white beams played around the room, struck his face. The two men recoiled abruptly.

'He's got a gun!' one of them cried, and fired his pistol.

Neville heard the bullet smash into the wall over his head. Then the pistol was jolting in his hand, splashing his face with bursts of light. He didn't fire at any one of them; he just kept pulling the trigger automatically. One of the men cried out in pain.

Then Neville felt a violent club blow across his chest. He staggered back, and jagged, burning pain exploded in his body. He fired once more, then crashed to his knees, the pistol slipping from his fingers.

'You got him!' he heard someone cry as he fell on his face. He tried to reach out for the pistol but a dark boot stamped on his hand and broke it. Neville drew in his hand with a rattling gasp and stared through pain-glazed eyes at the floor.

Rough hands slid under his armpits and pulled him up. He kept wondering when they would shoot him again. Virge, he thought, Virge, I'm coming with you now. The pain in his chest was like molten lead poured over him from a great height. He felt and heard his boot tips scraping over the floor and waited for death. I want to die in my own house, he thought. He struggled feebly but they didn't stop. Hot pain raked saw-toothed nails through his chest as they dragged him through the front room.

'No,' he groaned. 'No!'

Then pain surged up from his chest and drove a barbed club into his brain. Everything began spinning away into blackness.

'Virge,' he muttered in a hoarse whisper.

And the dark men dragged his lifeless body from the house. Into the night. Into the world that was theirs and no longer his.

CHAPTER TWENTY-ONE

Sound; a murmured rustle in the air. Robert Neville coughed weakly, then grimaced as the pain filled his chest. A bubbling groan passed his lips and his head rolled slightly on the flat pillow. The sound grew stronger, it became a rumbling mixture of noises. His hands drew in slowly at his sides. Why didn't they take the fire off his chest? He could feel hot coals dropping through openings in his flesh. Another groan, agonized and breathless, twitched his graying lips. Then his eyes fluttered open.

He stared at the rough plaster ceiling for a full minute without blinking. Pain ebbed and swelled in his chest with an endless, nerve-clutching throb. His face remained a taut, lined mask of resistance to the pain. If he relaxed for a second, it enveloped him completely; he had to fight it. For the first few minutes he could only struggle with the pain, suffering beneath its hot stabbing. Then, after a while, his brain began to function; slowly, like a machine faltering, starting and stopping, turning and jamming gears.

Where am I? It was his first thought. The pain was awful. He looked down at his chest and saw that it was bound with a wide bandage, a great, moist spot of red rising and falling jerkily in the middle of it. He closed his eyes and swallowed. I'm hurt, he thought. I'm hurt badly. His mouth and throat felt powdery dry. Where am I, what am I . . .

Then he remembered; the dark men and the attack on his house. And he knew where he was even before he turned his head slowly, achingly, and saw the barred windows across the tiny cubicle. He looked at the windows for a long time, face tight, teeth clenched together. The sound was outside; the rushing, confused sound.

He let his head roll back on the pillow and lay staring at the ceiling. It was hard to understand the moment on its own terms. Hard to believe it wasn't all a nightmare. Over three years alone in his house. Now this.

But he couldn't doubt the sharp, shifting pain in his chest and he couldn't doubt the way the moist, red spot kept getting bigger and bigger. He closed his eyes. I'm going to die, he thought.

He tried to understand that. But that didn't work either. In spite of having lived with death all these years, in spite of having walked a tightrope of bare existence across an endless maw of death – in spite of that he couldn't understand it. Personal death still was a thing beyond comprehension.

He was still on his back when the door behind him opened.

He couldn't turn; it hurt too much. He lay there and listened to footsteps approach the bed, then stop. He looked up but the person hadn't come into view yet. My executioner, he thought, the justice of this new society. He closed his eyes and waited.

The shoes moved again until he knew the person was by the cot. He tried to swallow but his throat was too dry. He ran his tongue over his lips.

'Are you thirsty?'

He looked up with dulled eyes at her and suddenly his heart began throbbing. The increased blood flow made the pain billow up and swallow him for a moment. He couldn't cut off the groan of agony. He twisted his head on the pillow, biting his lips and clutching at the blanket feverishly. The red spot grew bigger.

She was on her knees now, patting perspiration from his brow, touching his lips with a cool, wet cloth. The pain began to subside slowly and her face came into gradual focus. Neville lay motionless, staring at her with pain-filled eyes.

'So,' he finally said.

She didn't answer. She got up and sat on the edge of the bed. She patted his brow again. Then she reached over his head and he heard her pouring water into a glass.

The pain dug razors into him as she lifted his head a little so he could drink. This is what they must have felt when the pikes went into them, he thought. This cutting, biting agony, the escape of life's blood.

His head fell back on the pillow.

'Thank you,' he murmured.

She sat looking down at him, a strange mixture of sympathy and detachment on her face. Her reddish hair was drawn back into a tight cluster behind her head and clipped there. She looked very clean-cut and self-possessed.

'You wouldn't believe me, would you?' she said.

A little cough puffed out his cheeks. His mouth opened and he sucked in some of the damp morning air.

'I . . . believed you,' he said.

'Then why didn't you go?'

He tried to speak but the words jumbled together. His throat moved and he drew in another faltering breath.

'I . . . couldn't,' he muttered. 'I almost went several times. Once I even packed and . . . started out. But I couldn't, I couldn't . . . go. I was too used to the . . . the house. It was a habit, just . . . just like the habit of living. I got . . . used to it.'

Her eyes ran over his sweat-greased face and she pressed her lips together as she patted his forehead again.

'It's too late now,' she said then. 'You know that, don't you?'

Something clicked in his throat as he swallowed.

'I know,' he said.

He tried to smile but his lips only twitched.

'Why did you fight them?' she said. 'They had orders to bring you in unharmed. If you hadn't fired at them they wouldn't have harmed you.'

His throat contracted.

'What difference . . .' he gasped.

His eyes closed and he gritted his teeth tightly to force back the pain.

When he opened them again she was still there. The expression on her face had not changed.

His smile was weak and tortured.

'Your . . . your society is . . . certainly a fine one,' he gasped. 'Who are those . . . those gangsters who came to get me? The . . . the council of justice?'

Her look was dispassionate. She's changed, he thought suddenly.

'New societies are always primitive,' she answered. 'You should know that. In a way we're like a revolutionary group – repossessing society by violence. It's inevitable. Violence is no stranger to you. You've killed. Many times.'

'Only to . . . to survive.'

'That's exactly why we're killing,' she said calmly. 'To survive. We can't allow the dead to exist beside the living. Their brains are impaired, they exist for only one purpose. They *have* to be destroyed. As one who killed the dead *and* the living, you know that.'

The deep breath he took made the pain wrench at his insides. His eyes were stark with pain as he shuddered. It's got to end soon, he thought. I can't stand much more of this. No, death did not frighten him. He didn't understand it, but he didn't fear it either.

The swelling pain sank down and the clouds passed from his eyes. He looked up at her calm face.

'I hope so,' he said. 'But . . . but did you see their faces when they . . . they killed?' His throat moved convulsively. 'Joy,' he mumbled. 'Pure joy.'

Her smile was thin and withdrawn. She *has* changed, he thought, entirely.

'Did you ever see *your* face,' she asked, 'when you killed?' She patted his brow with the cloth. 'I saw it – remember? It was frightening. And you weren't even killing then, you were just chasing me.'

He closed his eyes. Why am I listening to her? he thought. She's become a brainless convert to this new violence.

'Maybe you did see joy on their faces,' she said. 'It's not surprising. They're young. And they *are* killers – assigned killers, legal killers. They're respected for their killing, admired for it. What can you expect from them? They're only fallible men. And men can learn to enjoy killing. That's an old story, Neville. You know that.'

He looked up at her. Her smile was the tight, forced smile of a woman who was trying to forgo being a woman in favor of her dedication.

'Robert Neville,' she said, 'the last of the old race.'

His face tightened.

'Last?' he muttered, feeling the heavy sinking of utter loneliness in him.

'As far as we know,' she said casually. 'You're quite unique, you know. When you're gone, there won't be anyone else like you within our particular society.'

He looked toward the window.

'Those are . . . people . . . outside,' he said.

She nodded. 'They're waiting.'

'For my death?'

'For your execution,' she said.

He felt himself tighten as he looked up at her.

'You'd better hurry,' he said, without fear, with a sudden defiance in his hoarse voice.

They looked at each other for a long moment. Then something seemed to give in her. Her face grew blank.

'I knew it,' she said softly. 'I knew you wouldn't be afraid.'

Impulsively she put her hand over his.

'When I first heard that they were ordered to your house, I was going to go there and warn you. But then I knew that if you were still there, nothing would make you go. Then I was going to try to help you escape after they brought you in. But they told me you'd been shot and I knew that escape was impossible too.'

A smile flitted over her lips.

'I'm glad you're not afraid,' she said. 'You're very brave.' Her voice grew soft. 'Robert.'

They were silent and he felt her hand tighten on his.

'How is it you can . . . come in here?' he asked then.

'I'm a ranking officer in the new society,' she said.

His hand stirred under hers.

'Don't . . . let it get . . .' He coughed up blood. 'Don't let it get . . . too brutal. Too heartless.'

'What can I—' she started, then stopped. She smiled at him. 'I'll try,' she said.

He couldn't go on. The pain was getting worse. It twisted and turned like a clutching animal in his body.

Ruth leaned over him.

'Robert,' she said, 'listen to me. They mean to execute you. Even though you're wounded. They have to. The people have been out there all night, waiting. They're terrified of you, Robert, they hate you. And they want your life.'

She reached up quickly and unbuttoned her blouse. Reaching under her brassiere, she took out a tiny packet and pressed it into his right palm.

'It's all I can do, Robert,' she whispered, 'to make it easier. I warned you, I *told* you to go.' Her voice broke a little. 'You just can't fight so many, Robert.'

'I know.' The words were gagging sounds in his throat.

For a moment she stood over his bed, a look of natural compassion on her face. It was all a pose, he thought, her coming in and being so official. She was afraid to be herself. I can understand that.

Ruth bent over him and her cool lips pressed on his.

'You'll be with her soon,' she murmured hastily.

Then she straightened up, her lips pressed together tightly. She buttoned the two top buttons of her blouse. A moment longer she looked down at him. Then her eyes glanced at his right hand.

'Take them soon,' she murmured, and turned away quickly.

He heard her footsteps moving across the floor. Then the door was shutting and he heard the sound of it being locked. He closed his eyes and felt warm tears pushing out from beneath the lids. Good-by, Ruth.

Good-by, everything.

Then, suddenly, he drew in a quick breath. Bracing himself, he pushed himself up to a sitting position. He refused to let himself collapse at the burning pain that exploded in his chest. Teeth grating together, he stood up on his feet. For a moment he almost fell, but, catching his balance, he stumbled across the floor on vibrating legs he could hardly feel.

He fell against the window and looked out.

The street was filled with people. They milled and stirred in the gray light of morning, the sound of their talking like the buzzing of a million insects.

He looked out over the people, his left hand gripping the bars with bloodless fingers, his eyes fever-lit.

Then someone saw him.

For a moment there was an increased babbling of voices, a few startled cries.

Then sudden silence, as though a heavy blanket had fallen over their heads. They all stood looking up at him with their white faces. He stared back. And suddenly he thought, I'm the abnormal one now. Normalcy was a majority concept, the standard of many and not the standard of just one man.

Abruptly that realization joined with what he saw on their faces – awe, fear, shrinking horror – and he knew that they *were* afraid of him. To them he was some terrible scourge they had never seen, a scourge even worse than the disease they had come to live with. He was an invisible specter who had left for evidence of his existence the bloodless bodies of their loved ones. And he understood what they felt and did not hate them. His right hand tightened on the tiny envelope of pills. So long as the end did not come with violence, so long as it did not have to be a butchery before their eyes . . .

Robert Neville looked out over the new people of the earth.

He knew he did not belong to them; he knew that, like the vampires, he was anathema and black terror to be destroyed. And, abruptly, the concept came, amusing to him even in his pain.

A coughing chuckle filled his throat. He turned and leaned against the wall while he swallowed the pills. Full circle, he thought while the final lethargy crept into his limbs. Full circle. A new terror born in death, a new superstition entering the unassailable fortress of forever.

I am legend.

AFTERWORD
by Stephen King

To say that Richard Matheson invented the horror story would be as ridiculous as it would be to say that Elvis Presley invented rock and roll – what, the purist would scream, about Chuck Berry, Little Richard, Stick McGhee, The Robins, and a dozen others? The same is true in the horror genre, which is the equivalent of rock and roll – a quick hit to the head that bobs your nerves and makes hurt so good.

Before Matheson came dozens, going back to the author of the Grendel story, and Mary Shelley, and Horace Walpole, and Edgar Allan Poe, and Bram Stoker, and H.P. Lovecraft, and . . .

But like rock and roll, or any other genre that skates across the nerve-endings, horror must constantly regenerate and renew itself or die.

In the early 1950s, when *Weird Tales* was dying its slow death and Robert Bloch, horror's greatest writer at the time, had turned to psychological tales (and at this same time Fritz Leiber, easily Bloch's equal, had fallen oddly silent for a time) and the genre was languishing in the horse latitudes, Richard Matheson came like a bolt of pure ozone lightning.

He single-handedly regenerated a stagnant genre, rejecting the conventions of the pulps which were already dying, incorporating sexual impulses and images into his work as Theodore Sturgeon had already begun to do in his science fiction, and writing a series of gut-bucket stories that were like shots of white lightning.

What do I remember about those stories?

I remember what they taught me; the same thing rock's most recent regenerator, Bruce Springsteen, articulates in one of his songs: No retreat, baby, no surrender. I remember that Matheson would never give ground. When you thought it *had* to be over, that your nerves couldn't stand any more, *that* was when Matheson turned on the afterburners and went into overdrive. He wouldn't quit. He was relentless. The baroque intonations of Lovecraft, the perfervid prose of the pulps, the sexual innuendoes were all absent. You were faced with so much pure drive that only re-readings showed Matheson's wit, cleverness, and control.

When people talk about genre, I guess they mention my name first, but without Richard Matheson, I wouldn't be around. He is as much my father as Bessie Smith was Elvis Presley's mother. He came when he was needed, and his stories hold all their original hypnotic appeal.

Be warned: You are in the hands of a writer who asks no quarter and gives none. He will wring you dry . . . and when you close this volume he will leave you with the greatest gift a writer can give: He will leave you wanting more.

Richard Matheson was born in 1926. He began publishing SF with his short story 'Born of Man and Woman' which appeared in *The Magazine of Fantasy and Science Fiction* in 1950. *I Am Legend* was published in 1954 and has been adapted to film three times. Matheson wrote the script for the film *The Incredible Shrinking Man*, an adaptation of his second SF novel *The Shrinking Man* (published in 1956). The film won a Hugo award in 1958. He wrote many screenplays (including *The Fall of the House of Usher*) as well as episodes of *The Twilight Zone*. He continued to write short stories and novels, some of which formed the basis for film scripts, including *Duel*, directed by Steven Spielberg in 1971. Further SF short stories were collected in *The Shores of Space* (1957) and *Shock!* (1961). His other novels include *Hell House* (1971) (filmed as *The Legend of Hell House* in 1973), *Bid Time Return* (1975), *Earthbound* (1982) and *Journal of the Gun Years* (1992). A film of his novel *What Dreams May Come* (1978) was released in 1998, starring Robin Williams. A collection of his stories from the 1950s and 1960s was released in 1989 as *Richard Matheson: Collected Stories*.

SF MASTERWORKS

** no longer available